PSYCHO PUNKS

DOLLS AND DOUCHEBAGS PART FIVE

MADELINE FAY

To all the girlies in their dark romance era... this book is for you.
Look down.

.

.

.

.

.

.

.

.

.

.

.

Good Girl.

PROLOGUE

Jin

To be a smart man in business, you should always test whatever you're selling to make sure the quality is good. I'm not a stupid man though. I don't taste my product until someone else under my command does first. Every smart medieval king in the Renaissance had a taste tester to make sure his food was never poisoned. If his servant didn't drop dead, then he could fill his stomach with all the riches. I'm going to make sure I'll never go hungry, that my plate will overflow, and I'll throw the scraps to those beneath me.

Take that lowlife piece of shit, Cruz, for instance. I let him into my circle, gave him a little power, and he's eating right out of the palm of my hand. He came onto my turf, the city that's always been mine, just for a whore. He's at my disposal though. I set him up on my yacht, let him lay his head down on expensive feather pillows at night, but he doesn't know that the yacht he's using is the same one I use to ship out my girls across the ocean. He's nothing special. Thousands of girls trafficked slept on the same yacht he does, not knowing they would wake up in another country sold to another man. Cruz is just another pawn for me to control then destroy when I feel the time is right. So yes, I'll let him stay on my multimillion-dollar yacht, have the best bedding and service at his waiting hand and feet, because he's going to get to torture that whore who's taking over my son's life. When the time is right, I'll wipe it all away and have it cleaned for the next person on my chessboard.

"Sir." A throat clears at my open door, interrupting as I watch one of the new girls deeply inhale the line of pure white powder through her nose on the surface of my desk.

I draw my gaze away, groping her naked breast as she sways on her haunches near my feet as the drug takes effect. It works fast once it hits the bloodstream, leaving euphoria and bliss in its wake.

"Come," I command one of my triads in as he stands in the doorway, unsure since I don't always take business inside my house, but my fucking warehouse burned down and I'm not at the downtown China office today. His duty usually is to follow my daughter around discreetly, so there can only be one reason why he's here: "What has she done now?"

I watch him tug at his necktie, gulping loudly as he bows and steps into my office. In the last few days, I've been getting this reaction from all of my triads. Everyone is walking on eggshells around me since Dom's gang ruined my auction and burned my business to the ground. My fist slams down on the surface of my desk, making the girl at my feet yelp as she falls down on her naked ass. Every time I clear my head, thinking of anything else, the reminder that someone dared to embarrass me comes back swiftly, like a tsunami. Anger and destruction pulse through my veins, making my head pound with the need for vengeance. I still can't wrap my head around how Dom and his fucking gang knew where and when my auction was taking place.

Someone talked, and I will find out who; it's only a matter of time.

"She, uh, well... sir." I raise an eyebrow at his lack of words, wondering if I should just dispose of him since he's wasting my time.

"What!" I bark out, my patience going out the window the moment he stepped through my door.

"Nicola was seen walking into the residence of Dom. We didn't know at first it was his until he stepped outside with..." His face pales, and a bead of sweat rolls down his temple as he gets nervous the longer I glare at him to continue. "Nicholas and his friends were seen leaving the premises with that girl."

I don't move a muscle. My body strains to pick up my cell phone and have my son come to my house so I can slowly choke the life out of him. He's dead to me. I no longer have a son, and he'll regret the day he betrayed me, his own flesh and blood.

"Gather the men and continue to follow him. Bring me my daughter."

He bows and quickly turns on his heels to leave the room. The moment the door is shut, I sweep my hand over my desk, sending everything to the floor with a crash. My breathing is labored as I collapse back into my chair.

I no longer have a son or daughter. Nicholas is about to learn that no one, not even my own blood, can go behind my back. When he sees what I'll do to Nicola, he will wish I put a bullet through his head instead of making him watch as my men torture his sister before someone buys her.

My triad will destroy them all.

CHAPTER 1

Tillie

"*P*aris!" Logan shouts until his voice is hoarse, struggling with the chains until his whole body strains on the edge of his seat.

I collapse back in my chair, feeling numb and disoriented, like this isn't really happening. He's picking Paris. I thought after everything, the whispered words and promises... My vision blurs as tears cloud over my eyes.

"I knew you'd pick me, baby; we're meant to be together," Paris gushes as I turn my head to look at her, seeing her gloating expression at the devastation that must be mine.

"I pick Paris. Kill the bitch; I don't give a flying fuck what you do to her! Just let Tillie go! She hasn't done anything. Keep me, but let her go." Logan heaves for breath until his voice catches on a hitch. My head whips over to stare at him in disbelief.

Did he really say that?

He meets my stare head-on, his muscles tight and bulging as the chains pull taut. He struggles against the steel, almost like he's going to break out of them and take me away. I feel more tears collect, spilling down my cheeks, as he looks at me with so much love and heartbreak at the same time.

"I'm sorry, baby girl. I couldn't protect you like I promised," he whispers in a choked voice, his muscular shoulders slumping with defeat as his head bows down. Those chocolate locks I love to run my fingers through, blocking my view of his face,

"What?! You can't mean that! You can't kill me! Do you fuckers know who I am?" Paris goes ballistic next to me, her chair rocking side to side as she goes nuts to escape.

"You've chosen, but will you pull the trigger?" Evan steps into the doorway, covered in shadows and a black ski mask, as he talks into his collective Darth Vader voice box.

I would laugh, but I feel like my heart is going to burst out of my chest and land at Logan's feet in a bloody mess. I know he'll take care of me, keeping me close and protected. He really does love me, and I can't stop fucking crying.

This right here.

This fucking moment makes us stronger.

"I'll do whatever the fuck you want, but you let her go." Logan doesn't look away from Evan's hiding spot; his eyes are telling everyone that once he's free, everyone dies.

I practically swooned in my chair, blinking away tears. I'm going to love him so hard; by love, I mean with my whole heart and vagina. I'm going to hug his cock tight with my pussy while telling him I'm completely his.

I might be a bit crazy like Tey, but fuck it.

Mine.

Another shadow of a man steps into the room, and I look out of the corner of my eye, knowing right away that it's Dom. He has this confident swagger that can't be missed. It says, look at me; I hold the upper hand and have a big dick.

Ignoring the screeches of Paris, or at least trying to since it feels like she's screaming in my ear, I give Dom a small nod and watch him walk across the room to stand behind Logan.

My sexy Italian stops struggling right away, his whole body going rigid at having a man at his exposed back.

"There's one bullet in the gun; make the shot count." Evan's voice trembles slightly, and he quickly walks out the door beside him, leaving Dom to do the rest.

A gun is placed in Logan's chained hand; his arm only allows so much movement that he can't raise the weapon higher than his waist. It happens within the blink of an eye; he doesn't hesitate the moment his fingers grip the gun.

Click.

Click.

Click.

Logan repeatedly pulls the trigger, the empty sound of the gun echoing around the cement walls. His teeth are gnashing together as he lowers his arm and tosses the weapon at Paris's feet with a curse after he just had it pointed right between her eyes.

"You were really going to kill me! You motherfucker! My daddy will kill you for this. He knows people!"

This bitch.

I bet her "daddy" knows people, being the slimeball judge he is since he associates himself with Franco. Corrupted and evil, just like his "lovely" daughter.

"Knows people? Little girl, I am the people," Dom announces in a beautiful, haunting voice as he addresses Paris, breaking his silence and walking around to stand in front of Logan with his enormous arms crossed over his wide chest.

"You son of a bitch!" Logan starts cursing, his words

switching to Italian and back to English. I'm not sure he even notices he's doing that.

Dom pulls his mask off, and even with the light dim, I can see him roll his eyes as he ignores Logan. His steps are slow as he comes over to my sitting position and trails his fingers around my neck and down my shoulder so lightly that I shiver.

"My daddy's a powerful man! You'll go missing, and no one will miss you! I'll tell him to kill you!" Paris continues to scream, but I block her out as shivers from Dom's sensual touch trail down my spine.

I meet Logan's angry eyes but see the hurt behind the mask he's trying to put on. My strong, broken man contains so much pain. I only want to take it all away for him and see him open up to me completely.

I think he can do that once he understands why I did it. Maybe he already does, but I'll prove to him that nothing can ever break us apart now.

I'm all in.

"Have fun, mama. Try not to make him bleed too much," Dom mutters smoothly into my ear, that slight Spanish accent turning my insides to freaking jelly.

I have it really bad for these men. I was doomed from the very beginning, the moment we all met, but that's okay. One way or another, we live and breathe until, one day, we just stop. I'd rather have my last breath knowing that I fucking lived to my fullest and loved to the point of pain.

It's worth all of it.

"I'll try," I whisper with a small chuckle and stand up the moment he cuts my zip ties, freeing my wrists.

I place a soft kiss on his whiskery cheek, loving the feel of his stubble against my lips, and drop back down on my heels. He smooths a large palm through my hair while pulling a loaded gun from the waistband of his pants and gently placing a gun in my right hand.

He kisses the top of my head with a small sigh, like he doesn't want to leave the room, but he pulls away and leaves with the door shutting behind him.

With a deep breath, I glance away from the doorway and gather my courage as my fingers grip the gun.

My eyes meet light brown, honey-colored eyes again. He stares at me without blinking, his wide, strong chest rising and falling rapidly while his lips are pressed in a tight line. So that's how it's going to be? He's not going to break the silence first.

Without looking away, I tug my underwear down my legs until they're pooling at my ankles. Logan's pupils widen; his face is set in stone, but his eyes betray him always, with so much emotion showing. Lust and anger are such beautiful looks on him. He could want to hate or kill me, but he'll never stop wanting me.

"I hope you're sold and raped a million times over!" Paris screeches, glaring death daggers at me when I look over at her.

She broke the silence between me and Logan.

God. I hate her.

I bend down, grab my panties, and take two steps to stand in front of her. I can feel Logan's gaze on my ass, making my insides burn alive with the heat from his stare.

"You should just shut up while you can. You're only digging your hole deeper," I say to Paris, staring down at her with disgust.

"Fuck you, cunt. You have no idea what I can have done to you!" Paris screams, her face turning an ugly shade of red.

I tsk at her and snap my hand out to grab ahold of her

cheeks between my pointer finger and thumb until her mouth drops open under the hard pressure.

"That's why you'll always be weak, Paris. I don't let anyone else do my dirty laundry. Now, since you can't shut up, I'll just have to make you. Watch and learn bitch, because you'll never have what's mine," I threaten darkly and quickly shove my balled up panties in her mouth. I chuckle as she gags and screams behind the fabric I shoved practically down her throat. She won't be able to spit them out.

With her jabbering mouth somewhat quiet, I pivot on my feet and try to appear calm as I approach Logan. Stepping between his spread thighs, I stare into his intense eyes and slowly lower to my knees until my eyes are at a level with his cock that's straining against his boxer briefs.

"I told myself no man would ever get me to willingly lower my knees to the floor. Ever. But here I am, right in front of you, on my fucking knees. Be mad all you want, but listen to what I have to say. Every single word that's going to come out of my mouth." My voice is raspy and slightly shaky as I hold his stare.

I place the gun down next to his feet, nervously running my hands lightly up and down his calves, hoping he'll understand.

He doesn't try to shove me away or say anything. His whole body is tense, but his eyes narrow sharply down at me as his nostrils flare when I feel tears gathering at the corner of my eyes.

"I was shut down for a long time, baby. Everything felt hollow, as if nothing mattered. I didn't hear or see anything. I raced to feel something for those split seconds, but it always ended the moment the rush died down. I went around like a ghost, Logan. I was so close to calling it quits…" He shakes his head angrily, his fists opening and closing like he wants to reach for me.

"Baby girl–" He swallows hard, but I stop him with a choked laugh, surprising him as his eyes widen.

"Let me finish." I shake my head, blinking the tears away as he slowly nods. "Then, I ran. I thought running and never stopping would make the demons stay away. The thing is, I still felt nothing. Until you. Dalton. Tey. Nicky. Dom. I'm so alive, Logan, that sometimes it's hard to catch my breath. Suddenly, I'm craving to be touched. To receive pain that's only going to end up in pleasure. It opened up a world to me that I never thought I'd have. It was as if I was looking outside behind a closed window, and then suddenly, I was on the other side and could taste freedom." I take a deep breath and pause from stroking his thighs the moment I reach the tight muscles, laying my palms flat to feel his strength.

"I forgave you. I put my heart at your feet, even though I knew you could break it. The only thing I held onto was my trust. It was on a leash so tight that it kept pulling me back. All this…" I glance around at Dom's torture room and glance back at Logan to see him so still that it looks like he's hardly breathing. "I'm fucking selfish, baby. I was testing you. All of this was a test to see if I could trust you, but you want to know something?" I whisper, convinced he's going to look at me differently, but I don't care.

"What?" He breathes raggedly, his body straining against the chains as he leans his face down toward me.

"If you would have pointed that gun at me and pulled the trigger, I would have still loved you. Me and you, Logan… There is no stopping this. I'm yours, and you're mine," I confess, rising on my knees to meet him halfway, his expression giving nothing away, so I can't tell what he's thinking.

"Say it again." He growls, his eyes hard and completely on me, as if I'm all he can see.

"Yours," I breathe out and watch in rapture as he slowly closes his eyes and exhales through his nose, his shoulders relaxing.

"Jesus. Fuck. Come here," he commands, snapping his eyes open and pulling his chains so hard that they rattle and cut into his wrists.

Gripping the back of his neck, I close the distance between us and slam my mouth roughly against his with everything I have. My teeth bite down on his bottom lip, drawing blood as it smears across our mouths when he angles his head the other way to deepen the kiss. Mint, something deep and dark like aged whiskey, and copper tingle on my tongue as he strokes his against mine. I'm drowning in him, and I hope I sink to the very bottom until I can't find my way out. As long as I can stay right here with him.

"I need you on my cock, baby girl. Now," he demands harshly, the deep timber in his voice literally making my thighs quiver.

We both ignore the muffled sounds coming from behind me as I sit back on my heels with a smirk. He tries to grab me, but he's pulled up short by the chains. He growls in frustration, and his upper lip curls in a snarl.

I love this side of him. Consumed by need, he gets demanding and so intense that I could choke on it.

"Unchain me," he commands, breathing heavily.

I slowly shake my head and slide my hands up his strong thighs, humming in admiration just before I reach the waistband of his boxers.

"No," I say simply, slowly pulling down the tight fabric

that molds to his tight, toned body until his big cock springs free and slaps against his abs.

Thick, long, and so hard, his cock looks painful as a drop of pre cum drips at his tip. Shiny and creamy. Fucking delicious, and all for me.

"No? Tillie, unchain me right the fuck now," he hisses as I lean forward while holding his gaze, his cock jerking as my tongue glides up his girthy length until I'm slowly licking the pre cum away at the fat tip of his beautiful cock.

More cum comes out as I keep taking my time licking his hard cock, moaning loudly as the salty taste of him explodes on my tongue.

"You're mine too, Lo. My slut. Now, be a good boy and let me worship you." I withdraw, bending my head back to stare up at him, loving every second of seeing the burning need in his eyes, his tight muscles bulging against his restraints, and the bead of sweat rolling down between his pecs.

"Fuck," he groans, squeezing his eyes shut tight and exhaling loudly.

His arms go slack at his sides as he spreads his knees wider apart, so I can fit perfectly between his thighs.

"Moothr fukr."

The muffled shouts from Paris cause me to chuckle, my hot breath washing over Logan's pulsing cock. He jerks in his seat and flashes his eyes open to see me already staring right at him, inches from his cock. Without looking away, I lick from root to tip so fucking slowly that I can feel the vein on his perfect cock thumping under my tongue.

"Shitttt. Baby girl, that feels amazing," he groans out loud, completely at my mercy, and stares at me like I'm the only thing he can see.

"Yeah? How about this?" I ask in a sultry voice as my tongue circles his engorged tip, collecting pre cum that leaves a string from my mouth to his cock when I slightly pull away to show him the white, sticky cum on the end of my tongue.

He inhales sharply, his nostrils flaring as his pupils dilate with uncontrollable desire. Just as I like him. Full of need and desperate, letting go of control for me.

"Good boy," I mutter before opening my mouth wide and sliding half his cock between my lips while hollowing my cheeks to suck the soul out of him.

He jumps in his chair, cursing in Italian and groaning so loudly that it seems to echo off the walls. I bob my head over his lap a few times, wetting his whole cock with drops of my saliva. Breathing through my nose and squeezing his thighs until my nails dig into his skin, I sink further down on him while flattening my tongue on the underside of his cock.

Why does it make me feel like a goddess, feeling the pumping of his heartbeat pick up on his cock? Every twitch and jerk as I swallow more of him until he's in the back of my throat and he's going insane above me.

"Jesus fucking Christ!" he shouts in a raspy voice, the chains rattling as his body jerks to reach for me again, and I stop sucking, looking up at him under my lashes with an arched brow.

If my mouth wasn't so full of him, on the verge of choking on his fat cock, I'd be smiling as he makes a sound of agony as he slumps back in his chair with his head thrown back. I love seeing his Adam's apple bobbing and the sheen of sweat slicking his skin. All mine. I slide my hands up his thighs, over the grooves of his hip bones, and up his muscled chest. Lightly skimming my fingertips over his throat and down his sternum, he chuckles at the pure adoration in my touch and glances back at me.

"God damn it, baby girl. You are killing me. Worship me

more," he pleads, swallowing hard as I drag my mouth off him while swirling my tongue the whole time until it's just the very tip.

I can't help sucking his unbelievably hard cock like a damn lollipop, feeling more pre cum collect on my tongue before slipping him from my mouth with a pop.

"Would you do anything for me?" I whisper, pulling away and standing up in front of him.

He watches my every movement as I reach back and unhook my bra, letting the fabric drop to the floor. I'm being devoured and ravished with just his eyes alone, and it's making my body burn for him.

"Anything," he simply states, not hesitating once.

I bend down and grab the gun, placing it in his hand before drawing back.

"Would you kill–"

A bang goes off, the warm splatter of blood hitting my naked back.

"–for me," I finish, breathing hard as he lowers the gun, dropping it on the floor.

I don't turn away from his penetrating gaze, but the sudden silence says enough.

One single step and I'm in his lap, my hands roaming over his broad shoulders before traveling up to sink in the back of his hair in a tight grip as I drag his mouth to mine.

I taste blood; the impact from kissing him so hard cuts one of our mouths. That's how it always is with this man.

Bloody.

Raw.

And dirty.

I hope it's always like this.

Shifting my hips back and forth over his lap, wetness

drips from between my legs, coating his whole cock until I can't take it anymore.

Pulling back, I inhale a deep breath and stare into his eyes as I reach down to grab his hard cock. Lining him up, I don't waste another second. I angle my hips and slam down on him, a cry leaving my lips. It feels like the best kind of pleasure and pain, and it makes me desperate for more. The sweet, delicious spread that makes my pussy weep for him as he practically tears me apart with his fat cock.

"You're fucking perfect. You know that?" he breathes out in awe, his voice rough, as I grip his shoulders and slide unhurriedly up his thick cock before pausing. "Ride me. Use me, baby girl. I'm all yours," he rasps out, holding completely still even as his cock jerks inside of me.

"Would you love me no matter what?" I ask, my legs trembling with the need to sink back down on him, but I need to hear it first.

"Always," he says easily, staring deeply into my eyes, that I finally let go.

I drop back down on him with a moan, loving the feeling of him filling me up, before rising back up to do it again. The wet, slick noise makes him groan as my pussy grips him tightly, dripping all over his cock. I love seeing his eyes half-closed with desire and the way his teeth clench as he tries to hold himself back from coming.

"Not yet," I demand with a long, drawn out moan.

"Fuck." He pants as I grind down on him, moving back and forth so that his pelvic bone rubs against my clit each time I push back against his hard, sweaty body.

My stomach tightens, feeling exquisite rapture gather and expand until my pussy is fluttering around his cock. Needing more, I lean back with my hands behind me on his knees and shift slowly with a roll of my hips. We both watch as his cock slips in and out of my pussy, glistening. He hits a spot inside of me that causes my toes to curl, and I move faster against him like my life depends on it. My thighs start to tremble; I'm close to coming. The sound of our breathing is loud, along with the filthy noise of his slicked cock rutting into me as he lifts his hips and fucks me hard. Supporting my hand on his thigh, I lean up slightly and grab the back of his neck with my other hand and slowly roll my hips over him. His full lips part as he stares at me, looking deep into my soul.

This is what it means when you find your other half—the one that completes you.

It starts with affection and turns into heartbreak, but somehow you find yourself falling in so deep that it's more than love.

It's a soulmate.

"Logan." My voice shakes, and I pant as I move faster and faster against him.

"I know, baby girl. I feel it too." His lips curl slightly with the smallest smile, feeling the same thing I am right now.

"Mine," I state this, sitting up to lean my forehead against his and wrap both arms around his neck.

"Yours." He groans, rolling his forehead along mine as he stares into my eyes without looking away.

"Oh God. Now, Lo." My pussy squeezes him tight, so tight that he has to muscle his cock in as if I'm trying to push him out until he's straight up rutting into me.

My screams pierce the walls, echoing back to us as my pussy walls flutter madly around him. Everything goes hazy. Only his honey eyes are my focus as I come and keep coming on his pulsing cock. Jerking back, his cock slips out of me, and the first wet splash hits his abs as I squirt again and again until it seems like it will never stop. He groans loudly and almost seems hypnotized as he watches his thick cock slip between my pussy lips until I'm completely stretched around him.

I slam down on him until he fills me so deeply that it almost hurts, and I stay that way as tiny aftershocks of my orgasm make me shake. The first splash of his cum actually makes me gasp; I can feel it every time more hot cum coats my insides. It seems endless, like he's never going to stop coming, even as it leaks out of me and drips between us.

"Fuck me." Logan pants, his cock still jerking inside of me.

I can't help laughing, even though I moan as I sit back on his lap with my arms around his neck and my fingers lazily sliding through his hair.

"I just did, and you were such a good boy." I smirk as he shifts his legs, making my body slide forward until I'm plastered against his chest.

He kisses me hungrily, owning my lips as he bites down on my bottom lip to hold me still as he growls. My eyes flutter shut in bliss as I deepen the kiss, never wanting it to end. His cock that was already semi-hard is at full mast again, and I can't help rocking my hips a little over the thick length of him.

"Peaches, I am in awe of you for putting our boy in his place. Also, I'm as hard as a fucking diamond. I recorded the whole thing for later. Spank bank, baby." Tey's voice echoes around the room, and I break the kiss, looking around for him until I notice the black speaker attached to the ceiling right next to a camera.

"I'm going to murder him." Logan groans, glaring up at the camera.

"Bad, Logan. Be a good boy, and the person with the key

might be willing to release you." Tey's voice is cut off as he chuckles like an evil villain.

Logan rolls his eyes and looks at me with a small smirk, saying, "I could think of worse places to be. I'm actually content right where I'm at."

"As much as I'd love to sit on your dick all day, I'd rather do it in a bed and not in Dom's torture basement with a dead body behind me." I remind him of Paris just as the main door to the room slides open.

"Enjoying yourself, mama?" Dom asks smoothly in that sexy, deep-accented voice of his as he walks over behind Logan and unlocks his chains with the key he produces from his pocket. "I must say, you look like the queen I know you are."

"Her throne of cocks. She rules over all our cocks and hearts, of course," Tey announces cheerfully while he literally skips into the room and stops right beside me to lay a smacking kiss on my cheek while trailing his fingers up and down my blood-covered back.

"Damn, little bitch." Dalton whistles in the doorway, taking in my position, then glancing behind me with a tilt of his head and saying, "You blow her brains out, bro? The last thing she saw was Tillie taking your dick like she owns it." He winks at me as he leans against the doorframe with his arms crossed over his barrel chest.

"Can I please take Paris's body for a while? I promise to have her parts back in time for Franco's dinner party." Tey pouts dramatically and bats his lashes when I look up at him, confused.

"What... Jesus. I forgot about the dinner with the judge. He's going to be in for a surprise, that's for sure." I glance over my shoulder and can't help but grimace at Paris.

Her body is still in a sitting position, but her head hangs

back with her chin tipped toward the ceiling. A bullet hole is just slightly below her jaw, and behind her on the wall is splattered brain matter. What a mess.

"I am not cleaning that up," I say with a shiver.

"What are you going to do with her body?" Nicky asks in a bored tone as he casually strolls into the room and stops by Paris's body.

He examines her as an excited Tey walks over to him and tilts her body parts left and right, like he can't decide where to start. Nicky tenses with a scowl on his face, and dare I say a hint of jealousy is shining in his green eyes?

"Nicholas," I say softly as I stand from Logan's lap with his helping hand, hiding my shaking limbs as best as I can and the cum leaking down my thighs while walking toward Nicky.

I'm not doing the best either since everyone's attention is on me like sharks in blood-infested water.

"Down boys." I giggle at the hungry looks scanning up and down my body. "What art piece are you going to make, TeyTey?" I ask with an interested hum as I twine my fingers with Nicky's and give him a gentle squeeze.

His whole body seems to melt with the simple touch, and his emerald eyes stare down at me with gratitude.

I get where he's coming from. Having to watch Tey from a distance and wanting him for so long, it's hard to get past the thought of him being someone else's, even a dead body. I'm the exception, and I'm just happy his heart is big enough for two people. I really do feel lucky every morning when I open my eyes and think about each of my guys.

"I was thinking the hole in the back of her head could be filled with flowers. I think it would be pretty." Tey circles Paris's body with his index and thumb cradling his chin as he's deep in thought.

That's my man. The artist.

"That's perfect," I say with approval in my voice and mean every word.

Whatever they do, I can't help but think that they are perfect in their own unique way, no matter if it looks crazy to the outside world.

What the hell does that say about me, though?

Crazy is, as crazy does?

Oh, well.

I joined the crazy train a long time ago.

Nicola

I love my brother, I really do, but I'm not about to watch him as he stares at the monitoring screen of Dom's torture chamber while my bitch best friend is fucking her other boyfriend into submission. It's really distracting listening to the moaning and a shit ton of dirty talk. It's why I'm in the back of the room with Evan as he faces the wall and hums under his breath to block out all the noise.

I think I'm in love. He's such a wonderful boyfriend, so caring and sweet, that I want to get out of here so I can ride his disco stick, but I'm going to have to wait. I don't want to listen to Tillie having sex, but I want to make sure she's okay. That's what friends do. Ride or die, or in this case, listen to my home girl get some.

That's my bestie in there, staking her claim, and I'm so damn proud of her.

"Girl power!" I shout loudly in the quiet surveillance room, interrupting the ragged breathing of her men and Tey's cray-cray mumbling.

Nicky whips his head over toward me, taking his dilated eyes off the computer screen. His eyebrows hit his hairline as if he's surprised, I'm still here and he forgot about me. I rock on my heels, pinch Evan's tight butt without meaning to, and shift my gaze to the ceiling because everyone is staring at me now and I'd rather not see the tented pants popping up everywhere I look.

Gross.

These guys are like big brothers to me. I've known them my whole life. Except Dom, so I guess it's okay to look. I mean, Tillie already gave me a mental image of what he's packing down there with her hands, so I'm kind of curious. It can't be bigger than Dalton's, and I only know his dick is big because I've always thought he walks a little too confidently as if he has a third leg, plus my girl was walking like a cowboy after I stumbled into their fuckfest at Gary the douche's party.

"Bonetown!" I yell, pointing fingers like little guns, and then smack myself in the forehead because it's now known what I was just thinking about.

I used to be beyond embarrassed by my Tourette's, but I learned over the years that no matter who you are, someone is always going to judge you. I decided to own that shit and make everyone else my bitch. Okay. Not really. I'm just a girl who looks in the mirror and likes what she sees. Not many can say or do that. We all have our flaws, differences, etc. I'm proud of mine.

"Jesus Christ, Nicola!" Nicky shouts in Japanese, striding quickly over me as he starts to steer me out of the room.

I only put up a little bit of a fight, digging my heels in until I hear Tillie over the speakers, "Would you love me no matter what?" Logan replies with "Always," and my job here is done. She's safe and damn happy, as far as I can tell from the screams coming through the speakers. I grab Evan's arm and pull him with me as Nicky walks us faster to the door. Once out in the hallway, Tillie's sounds of pleasure cut off as the surveillance room door shut behind us.

"Thank fuck," Evan mutters under his breath as his shoulders sag in relief.

He pushes his sexy glasses up his nose and grins at me with his Darth Vader helmet under his arm. So hot. I'm going to have him wear that later when I'm giving him a blow job. Ugh. I can totally picture him using Daddy Darth's voice to tell me he's my daddy.

The force of his orgasm will be strong.

I'm stuck daydreaming and shake my head when I see Nicky towering over my boyfriend.

"You got a problem with hearing my girl get fucked?" Nicky growls like a straight-up Neanderthal.

I quickly get between them, pushing on my big brother's chest, and flick him on the nose. He glares and takes a step back, crossing his arms with that annoying look on his face that says he's going to kill someone.

He's so weird.

"I could only handle singing 'Baby Shark Do Do Do' so much before I lost my mind. It's not easy blocking out all the noise going on in there, but I managed to." Evan stands up straighter, looking my brother in the eye without blinking, even though sweat is dripping down Evan's forehead the longer they stare at each other.

That's hot. He's totally getting a blowie after we get out of here for standing up to my overbearing brother.

Nicky narrows his eyes even more then he grunts before turning his gaze to me.

That's it. All is good now. Men are weird.

"Check in with me, keep your phone on you, and don't go home," Nicky grumbles, his facial expression worried, as he pulls me into a hug with a tight squeeze before letting me go.

My eyes water as I watch him disappear back into the room with the other guys. Nicky has always looked out for me. He shielded me from the harshness of the world we were born into and took the wrath of my father, so I was never harmed. My brother tried his hardest to keep me out of the way, and I pretended ignorance to appease him. I knew from an early age just how cruel our father was. I saw everything. Every beating Nicky received left bruises that he tried to hide from me and act like he wasn't in pain. The coming and going of evil men into our homes. The women would go into a building and not return. The dead look in my mother's eyes as she would quietly leave the room when my father became mad, letting his anger lash at Nicky.

I see it all, and it hurts so fucking much, knowing my brother suffers at the hands of our father. I lay in guilt at night, wondering what I can do to stop it all, but I sometimes think I'm weak like our mother. I never fight back because I'm afraid I'll end up like those girls who just disappear once they come across the triad. It all makes me want to scream at the top of my lungs and put a bullet through Jin's skull.

Maybe I can.

I can be strong and brave like Nicholas. Maybe it's finally my turn to protect him.

"Hey. What are you thinking about so hard over there?" Evan questions me as he drapes his arm over my shoulder while leading me out of the house and down the driveway to his car.

"Do you have a gun?" He jolts against me, startled by my answer, and looks into my eyes with his head tilted as his glasses slide down his nose.

Sexy, but in a nerdy way. I'm here for it.

I fidget in my seat the moment my butt hits the smooth leather. I'm trying to stay in control so my Tourette's doesn't get out of control as I watch him calmly shut my car door and round the hood.

He doesn't say anything as he starts the car and pulls out of the gate. His brows are pinched together in worry as he struggles to give me an answer. I end up smacking my arm repeatedly, not meaning to, as I become increasingly nervous the longer he's silent. My head twitches to the right in a tic that won't stop. Feeling his hand suddenly in mine helps my heart rate slow down, and I eventually can turn my head to look at him as the tics decrease.

"I have a concealed weapon. I'm just worried about why you're asking," Evan says, stroking his thumb back and forth over my wrist.

I won't ever lie to him. He's a good guy. He doesn't deserve deception from me. I sometimes wonder if love is worth dragging him into my dangerous world and if I'm only setting him up to get hurt, or worse, killed.

Love is funny that way. It can be selfish and hurt to the core because we don't want to lose the one good thing in our lives.

I guess I'm rotten, like Jin. I can't see my life without Evan's hand in mine.

"I'm going to kill my father. For Nicky and for myself," I say casually with a shrug like it's no big deal, but my palms sweat at just the thought of doing it.

Could I pull the trigger when the time came?

I don't know, but I have to try.

"Holy Batman!" he shouts out loud, making me jump in my seat as he lets go of my hand.

Evan swerves the car at the last second, realizing he ran

a stop sign and almost hit another car. Maybe I shouldn't be having this conversation while he's driving. I should have waited when we got to his house, distracted him with sex, and then announced I needed a bang stick. He straightens the wheel and takes a deep breath as he merges onto the highway toward his home, his gaze focused on the road.

"I'm thinking we might have to rethink this relationship," I start to say but screech as Evan yanks the wheel sharply, jumping over the intersection while I grab the 'oh shit' bar.

I bounce in my seat and gape at him as he quickly gets off the highway from the other side. Car horns honk at us; pissed-off drivers are probably praying for our deaths. For some reason, seeing him take control of the vehicle like that makes my vagina weep.

I need help. Like, someone should definitely call my therapist before I decide to give him road head and really get us in a car accident. He glances out of the corner of his eye at me, doing a double take since I'm staring at him twisted in my seat. I'm probably drooling, and my eyes keep shifting to his lap, wondering if his dick would like a warm hug from my mouth.

"You can't leave me. Me and you against the world, Nicola. I'll get you a fucking bazooka, grenades, or whatever you want. You just can't leave me," Evan says in a stern voice that I have to slap my hand when it climbs up my own leg to the promised land.

Fuck, that's hot.

His jaw is tight, his glasses perched on the end of his nose as he glares at the road, all while his knuckles turn white on the steering wheel.

"I love you." He curses at my declaration, nearly hitting an old lady who's crossing the street. "But if you let me finish talking, I was going to tell you Batman sucks. Go with Captain America next time. His ass is the symbol for America, after all."

He slams the brakes at the stoplight, jerking us both in our seats, and turns halfway toward me.

"You really mean that?" he chokes out, staring intensely at me.

Crap. Did I hurt his feelings? I literally have no filter.

"Your ass is so much better than Captain America, baby." I lean forward, petting his arm and making shushing noises to calm him down, just in case.

A car honks behind us, making Evan swear again as he notices the light green and turns forward again.

"No. Not that. You really love me?" He says this with a pitched voice before clearing his throat and looking over to see me nodding my head quickly.

"I love yo— Fuck!" I was leaning eagerly in my seat when I noticed his eyes shift over my shoulder and widen until I could only see his pupils expanding behind his glasses.

A loud crunch blasts in my ears, followed by shattering glass and screaming. It's so loud; that's all I can focus on as my world tips upside down. I'm the one making that noise, screaming in terror. Unbelievable pain spears into my shoulder and leg while my vision grows fuzzy. What seems like hours later but is probably only seconds later, I blink rapidly. The first thing I notice is that the windshield is scattered across the cement, and I'm hanging upside down.

Groaning, I slowly turn my head to see Evan hanging limply in his seat with blood dripping down his forehead.

"Evan." My voice comes out raspy and so quiet, probably from screaming and shock. "Evan!" I say loudly and sigh in relief as he groans in pain, blinking rapidly.

His glasses fell off at some point, so I know his eyesight is blurry and he can't see much. He's only looking at me, though, reaching his hand out frantically.

"You okay?!" He practically shouts, struggling in his seat, but his belt buckle won't come loose.

"Just dandy. What happened?" I look around, grimacing in pain at my burning shoulder, and notice multiple men, all dressed in black, heading our way with guns.

I whip my head toward Evan, seeing him clenching his ribs and breathing fast.

"I'm about to be taken, baby. Don't do anything. Tell Nicky the triad came to collect." I say it so fast I'm not even sure he understands, as he shakes his head as if to focus.

"Wha-What? No!" he yells, trying to reach for me as my mangled door is wrenched open and rough hands grab at me, cutting my seat belt loose.

"Nicola!" Evan screams at the top of his lungs as I'm dragged out, my legs cutting into the glass as my father's men grab me under my arms on each side.

The last thing I see is Evan's frantic eyes connecting with mine in despair before his body goes limp, probably passing out from blood loss.

I'm not even fighting; there isn't any point. The triad is surrounding Evan's car and the van I'm being tossed into. If my father was showing up, I would be thrown into a limo with his disapproving glare. This isn't the typical lecture that I'm a useless daughter; I'm being taken by my father's men and tossed around like yesterday's trash. I have the biggest feeling I'm going to be in a lot of pain later. I just hope my brother doesn't come for me and do anything stupid, like face Jin alone.

"Fuck!" I yell just as a burlap bag is thrown over my head

as I watch two of the triad walk back over to Evan and start to take him out of the car too.

No. No. No. No. Please, not Evan!

Please, Nicky. Don't come for me.

I repeat it over and over, wishing it would be true, but I know my brother.

We are both going to die.

CHAPTER 3

Tillie

"Precious..." a voice whispers low and wickedly in my ear. "Wakey wakey, Precious."

I groan and roll over, snuggling up against a warm, hard body just to get away from the most evil man in history. He comes after me anyway, wrapping an arm around my waist from behind, and strokes my belly over my satin pajamas.

"You can't escape me. Open those gorgeous eyes before I decide to pluck them out so I can stare at them all day," Tey whispers right into my ear like the devil, his hot breath causing goosebumps to pebble my arms.

His words register a second later, and my eyes snap open as I look over my shoulder at him to see his eyes crinkled at the corner from laughter but oh so serious.

"Jesus fucking Christ, Tey! It's too damn early for crazy talk. Either take her or shut the fuck up." Dalton's chest rumbles against my chest, his voice grumpy from being woken up before the sun decides to even rise.

"Take me? Really?" I mock his grumpy tone, glaring at him when I turn back toward Dalton, but he's already rolling away from me with an arm over his eyes before a snore sounds from his lush, parted lips.

"Great idea. I'm kidnapping you for the day. All mine. Whatever shall I do with you?" Tey whispers excitedly and makes me squeal as he tightens his arm around me, pulling me out of bed to scoop me in his arms, bridal style.

"You should put me back in bed, tuck me in, and tell me I'm pretty while going back to sleep," I sass, trying to glare, but it's hard when he's smiling so lovingly down at me.

He could be thinking I'm God's gift to him or taking my eyeballs to admire from a glass jar. I can never tell. Oh well, I know he loves me, so I'll take what I can get.

"Nope. But you are pretty. I like pretty things," he says, popping the P as he strides to the bathroom and sets me on the counter while petting my hair as if I'm a cute little puppy snuggled in his arms.

Without another word, he wets my toothbrush with toothpaste and hands it to me with an arched eyebrow, daring me to test him by disobeying his silent demand. I quickly brush my teeth with a groan, blurry-eyed, and wondering why I'm up so early. Last night was emotionally exhausting, but one of the best nights I can add to the growing list since meeting my guys. I broke Logan in the most beautiful ways, and he made me feel so complete that I never had to question his motives again. Never doubt us.

I feel so free and light. It's an odd feeling, but I never want to lose it.

I hop off the counter to rinse my mouth, glancing up at the mirror to see Tey leaning against the wall with his arms crossed and a soft smile. He looks peaceful and calm, which I haven't seen before. I go about washing my face, unable to keep my eyes off him for only a few seconds. Drying off, I spin around to him and wrap my arms around his waist, placing my chin on his chest while gazing up at him with a smile.

"Where are we going?" I try to put more of a chipper tone in my voice, needing to stay positive when I'd really like to crawl back into bed and ignore all my troubles.

"I want you to see how I grew up. I've seen all the bad and ugly in this fucked-up world, but not all of it is horrible. You shared everything with us, and I want to do the same," he says while swaying us in place, his smile contagiously spreading, that I can't help returning one of my own that doesn't feel forced.

"Whatever you want, baby." I reach up on my toes and peck a quick kiss on his cheek before separating from him to walk into my closet.

"Don't say things like that. I want a lot from you. Are you willing to give up your mind and body to me?" His voice is low, and his body is inches from my exposed back as I whip off Dom's t-shirt. I can see his shadow overtake mine in the dim lighting.

I don't say anything as I dress in soft, stretchy shorts and a loose tank top. I thought he would have understood by now, but I guess I have to actually say it. After the dungeon sex last night, I was carried up the stairs by Logan, and I could hear the guys following as they laughed and joked around. My freaking heart could have burst out of my chest and flopped around in joy. I have a family. Living a dangerous life takes a toll on you, but these moments of happiness are worth it.

Logan and Tey cleaned me thoughtfully in the warm shower without being too overly sexual. They took their sweet time, taking care of me after. It was the calming movements of their big hands that helped relax me while I helped wash off the blood splattered all over Tey's hands, all the way up to his elbows. After that, Lo picked me up again, like he couldn't bear to let me go even for a second.

Dom took his shirt off and placed it over my head the moment we emerged from the bathroom into the master suite, I could only smell the dark chocolate and spicy scent that was naturally his. We all gathered in the living room as I sat on Logan's lap sideways on the couch, and Dalton brushed my hair carefully through each tangle as I leaned my shoulder against his chest. No one brought up business or what the next day would hold; it was just light topics in hushed tones as a movie played in the background on low volume. I must have drifted off at some point because I didn't even wake up as I was placed in Dom's bed. I guess it's our bed now; we might need a bigger one to fit us all.

"I'd let you cut me open, bleeding just for you, until I'm drained and just an empty vessel. If it were my very last breath, I would die with a smile on my face because it's your face I'm seeing last with my blood smeared all over you. I'm all yours, Tey." I gasp as I find myself suddenly upside down. Tey has thrown me over his shoulder and is currently running out of the room with a manic laugh as I bounce against his shoulder.

"I love you so fucking much, Tillie. You have no idea," he says out of breath, running out the front door without shutting it.

"Jesus. Put me down!" My giggles can't be contained as he smacks my ass and stops by the garage doors that are opening just as he slides me down off his shoulder.

Everything spins until all I can see are Tey's bright blue eyes as he squishes my face between his hands.

"We have a surprise for you. I'm finally going to be your bitch!" Tey pumps his hands in the air and whistles just as the garage door opens.

Dom is leaning against a pitch-black crotch rocket with

his hands in his pockets and a broad grin. His white button-down shirt is open, leaving all his abs to my hungry gaze.

"Hey, mama." Dom's deep, accented Spanish voice feels like he caresses my skin, rubbing me in all the right ways. "Don't drive too fast, I don't want my queen hurt." He swaggers over me with cocky confidence as I bite my lip, looking him up and down. Is it hot in here? It should be illegal how good he looks as he places a pair of keys in my limp hand.

I can't believe this motorcycle is for me. My mouth drops in shock as I deny what's right in front of me. I look at the shiny surface of the bike that shows my reflection and back at Dom. My eyes don't know where to look first. Smooth, tan lines of Dom's abs as his shirt blows in the warm breeze, freaking looking like a Calvin Klein commercial, or the big smile stretching over Tey's face as he watches my head whip back and forth. I probably look like a cartoon character with my eyes wide and my mouth hanging open to catch flies.

"I-I don't know what to say! This is too much," I cry out, feeling a pinch in my chest, because I don't think I'll ever get used to surprises or presents.

"Don't say anything. Let us spoil you. We want to give you everything; accept it because it's too good for us, mama. It's worth seeing your eyes sparkle in warmth and joy." Dom holds my face between his large palms, placing a kiss on my forehead as light as a feather as he takes a deep breath.

"Stop sniffing her as if she's the best high you've ever had. Gimme! My turn!" Tey grumbles with a pout as his face appears next to ours; he's trying to wedge himself between us as if feeling left out.

I giggle, and a sensation like I'm floating comes over me. I want every day to be like this. No worries, no pressure—just us being, well, us. Almost normal.

Almost.

We'll never be normal like those people out there who get up in the morning with a smile and do the same thing every single day. Our lives will probably always be fireworks and explosions, but at least we can take them one step at a time. Days like today.

"Fine." I fake a sulky pout as if it's the worst thing ever to get a bike as a present.

Tey laughs and swings me around in a circle in his arms until I feel like I'm going to puke. Dizzy, he sets me down next to the bike and hops on, scooting back to make room for me in front of him. I'm excitedly jumping up and down, I can hardly wait to feel the thrill of driving fast and the bike vibrating between my legs. I'm just about to swing my leg over the small seat while grabbing the handlebars when a throat clears loudly behind me.

Spinning around, I skip back to Dom with a grin and stand on my toes with my hands sliding up his impressive chest until they rest against his broad shoulders. He stares down at me, a slow, pleased smile stretching across his handsome, tan face as he lowers his face to mine.

How the hell did I get so lucky landing men who are sexy as fuck? If I had a rosary, I'd be kissing the cross and thanking baby Jesus for sending me these dangerous, wicked men with muscles that I can admire and drool all over.

"I'm going to show you just how appreciative I am when we return," I emphasize by sliding my hand down to his belt and tugging at it, skimming my nails over the dips and ridges of his waist. "Thank you, *Papi*."

His nostrils flare as I slam our mouths together, flickering my tongue along his full bottom lip with a moan. He tastes like sin and dark chocolate. I'm addicted, my mouth fusing to his as he takes control of the kiss, sliding his big hand under my hair and gripping it tight. Angling his head, his tongue snakes against mine, stroke for stroke, lighting my body up and silently begging for more as I bite his lip. The growl that pushes up his throat has my pussy throbbing and my silk underwear drenched in seconds.

Am I forever going to walk around with wet panties around these men? I should probably carry around extra underwear, just in case.

"Be good." His tone is demanding yet smooth, with a throaty purr that promises more of his lips on my body later.

"Flower, I'm dying over here. My dick could cut granite. Please put me out of my misery," Tey groans behind us, and when I turn to walk back over to him, his arms are crossed over his chest, his black-painted nails tapping on his bicep as he pouts.

"Poor baby. Does it hurt?" I widen my eyes, straining not to smile as his eyes fill with actual tears.

"My balls are blue, Tillie. Blue! Help me?" he begs as one tear leaks down his sharp cheekbones, leaving a wet spot on his black t-shirt as it falls.

"I love you, but the fact you can produce tears this quickly scares me." I grab his hand as he uncrosses his arms and brings his finger up to my parted lips.

His eyes clear up real quick as I suck his index finger into my mouth, swirling my tongue around until I bite down hard enough to almost break skin while staring into his blue gaze. Releasing him with a pop, I lean forward and swipe my tongue up his cheek to catch a tear on his jaw. I hum under my breath and pull back with a wide grin at the glazed look in his eyes.

"I'm never letting you go. You can never hide; however far you run, I'll always find you." Tey draws in a deep breath, his nostrils flaring as he runs his tongue over his teeth, just as he grabs me around the waist and places me in front of him on the bike like I weigh next to nothing.

"Fuck." Dom drags a hand down his face and mutters something under his breath as he turns back to the garage door that leads into the house.

I can't help laughing wickedly, for I live to bring chaos and spice to their lives, and I'll always tease them. I start the bike, the engine vibration between my thighs as Tey plasters himself to my back, his cock grinding up against my ass as his breath warms my ear.

"You'll pay for that later. I bite back." His sinister tone holds a dark promise and I can't help shivering.

"I can hardly wait." I moan as I slowly press on the gas out of the garage, wondering why we aren't back in bed instead of pulling out of the gates and onto the road.

The moment we are out of the fancy, rich neighborhood, Tey points to the left. I follow his silent instructions without saying a word while pushing down on the gas so that the bike's front tire lifts slightly off the ground. Tey chuckles in my ear, his hands clenching my hips as the wind whips at our hair while I weave between cars at a neck-breaking speed.

I missed this. The sun on my skin, freedom always within reach. It's even better having Tey hold onto me as he howls like a wild animal into the wind.

***

Twenty minutes later, after Tey gave me directions by pointing each time we needed to turn, we were pulling into a run-down neighborhood. Some of the homes look abandoned, with dead grass on the front lawns, while others are littered with trash and fold-up lawn chairs. Not all of the houses are bad; we pass a home with an elderly lady sitting in a chair on her porch as she waves at us.

"Good morning, Rita!" Tey shouts out cheerfully; he must like her if he's being less of a psycho.

He points to a house at the end of the block—a faded yellow home with overgrown grass and a cracked driveway. I park us on the curb in front of the house and turn the bike off. Tey slides off the back and grabs my waist, lifting me off the seat before I even have a chance to swing my leg over. He hugs me to his chest, and I can't help but melt against him with my head resting right over where his heart is. The steady thump makes my shoulders relax. I hadn't even realized I was nervous about meeting people he cared about. Over the sound of his heart, I can hear the shouting of a couple a few houses down and the overexcited high shrieks of children playing in the backyard of Tey's foster home.

"Come on, sweets." Tey pulls back, running his hand over the top of my head with a grin that brings out the dimple on his left cheek.

Walking hand in hand to the front door, it opens before we can step onto the crumbling front porch.

"Tey! You're back!" a little boy shouts gleefully and launches himself into Tey's arms the moment we are standing in front of the door.

Tey lets go of my hand to catch the boy, who can't be older than five. They both laugh as Tey holds the kid to his side with one arm, his other hand rubbing small circles over his Superman t-shirt that has a few holes under the armpits.

"I said I would be. I always keep my promises, don't I, little man?" Tey tickles the kid's sides, making him wiggle and shriek in laughter.

I can't stop grinning; I love seeing Tey this way. He's good with kids, which is probably why he's constantly slipping in little hints that he wants to knock me up. He wants me barefoot and pregnant in the kitchen, or, in his case... in the dungeon. He can keep dreaming; I'm not even sure if I want kids. Me, a mother? I can picture a somewhat hazy image of a little girl with Tey's electric blue eyes and long black hair that resembles Nicky. It's impossible to get pregnant by two men at the same time, but that's all I'm seeing if I ever want to have a child. Dalton would be her protector, teaching her how to be independent while dressing up for tea parties if she demanded it. Logan would be stern but doting, to the point that she would be spoiled as hell. She'd be a little psycho like Tey, probably killing someone at the young age of six while Tey cheered her on with love shining in his gaze. Nicky would be bossy, creating a mini version of him. And my King, Dom, would treat her like a princess.

If it was a boy, I'd pray for him every night because he'd turn out just like his daddies.

My God.

We would all be doomed if we had children. They'd be monsters, but our little monsters. I can't believe I'm picturing this. Can I see myself being a mother?

Yeah, I think I can, but only with my guys by my side. I can't see myself raising a child with anyone else.

I'd teach my kid that it's okay to cry, to be happy, or to be angry. That if she or he falls, they can get right back up. I'll be there every step of the way.

I'm losing my mind over here, and I'm seconds away from having a panic attack. What the hell am I thinking? I'm not even out of high school yet.

Crap. I have baby on the brain, and I haven't even received a diploma. I'm too young to be a mom! Everyone just needs to chill here and take some deep breaths before I spiral into a panic attack. I think I'm the only one freaking out. This is all Tey's fault.

I try to distract my thoughts with something else so I don't end up attacking Tey and demanding he put a baby in me.

Think, Tillie. Think!

What is boring and not life-threatening at the moment... Ah! Got it! School.

I imagine my fist pumping in the air and patting myself on the back. School is a normal subject; everyone worries about it. Not me so much. It's better than being kidnapped, tortured, and kidnapped again. I'm probably not graduating now after missing so much fucking school. I used to be proud of that one thing I had control over before I came to California. Good grades are something I could say I achieved myself. Unless I pull a Dalton and just get my GED.

One step at a time. I have to remind myself.

Someone's always trying to kill me every few days; I deserve a freaking break. I'll worry about it later. Maybe Nicky can tutor me; he's too smart for his own good, plus he'll like bossing me around.

"Arthur, meet my gorgeous Tillie. Gorgeous, this is King Arthur," Tey introduces us with a grin, pulling me out of my crazy thoughts.

I'm about to say hi and ask the little guy if he thinks Tey is a good big brother since he seems great with children, but I quickly change my mind.

He holds Arthur away from his body and crouches just before he launches the kid in the air over his head. My heart fucking drops down to my ass as Arthur screams, looking like he's flying like Superman, so high up over Tey.

"Tey!" I shriek, clutching my chest in panic with both hands as I reach out as if to catch Arthur.

I breathe out a relieved sigh as Tey catches him, both of them turning their heads to look at me like I'm crazy for yelling and fluttering around them like a mother hen.

"Calm down, Til. We do this all the time. No one ever threw you up in the air?" Tey questions me, setting Arthur down on the driveway when he sees my worried expression.

I can't help but think the kid will end up in space with how high Tey was throwing him. Or break all his bones if he falls.

"Maybe don't toss kids around me like you're juggling them. Okay?" I choke out, watching as Arthur gives me a weird look as if I'm the crazy one, just before he takes off to run into the backyard.

"I promise not to throw kids around you anymore, precious," Tey coos, leading me into the house while rubbing my back in soothing circles.

I squint my eyes at him, noticing he didn't mention he wouldn't throw kids even if I wasn't around him. Smooth and easy words come off his tongue like silk. I can pretend I didn't know I was being lied to for peace of mind and all that jazz.

"Fucker," I hiss out of the corner of my mouth and pinch his side, hiding my own grin as he chuckles under his breath with a shrug.

Rolling my eyes, I look away to hide my amusement and take in the room we are standing in. Faded orange carpet that kind of smells a little like mildew covers the living room flooring, but at least it looks somewhat clean. I glance around, taking in the ninety's furniture and the peeling wallpaper in the dining room that I can see through a doorway. It's a small home, but it doesn't seem too bad. I've seen a lot worse. Two kids are playing a video game as they shove each other on the couch while yelling at the screen. The preteens completely ignore Tey and me as he leads me through a swinging wooden door into a kitchen.

Instantly, the smell of cigarettes and spoiled milk hits my nostrils, and my gaze snags on the baby bottles littering the counter. As for the smoke, it's coming from the woman sitting at the kitchen table, muttering under her breath as a cigarette dangles from her mouth. She ignores the whimpering baby in the high chair, focusing on the quarter she's using for a scratch-off.

Tey tenses next to me, his arm dropping from my back as he stalks forward on silent feet over to the older woman. I watch as he reaches behind his back, his shirt rising up to show the glint of his knife as he pulls it out of his belt with a quiet slick. I cross my arms and lean back against a counter to watch the show. The lady doesn't even know the danger she's about to find herself in. It's like watching a snake move silently and stealthily. If you suddenly move too quickly, it will strike viciously and fatally. Tey is at the stage of watching her with his head tilted to the side, a few steps away. Studying her.

I huff quietly under my breath, wondering if I need to search for a body bag around here. There's probably one in Tey's room, no doubt, but I wasn't really looking forward to helping him hide a body today.

Oh well. Beggars can't be choosers.

"Gloria," Tey says in a low voice, causing goosebumps to break out over my skin and causing Gloria to jump in her chair with a yelp. "Tell me you haven't been ignoring Izzy for a scratch-off you'll never win."

Menacing.

That's the energy currently surrounding Tey.

"N-No. I was, uh, just about to feed her." Gloria bangs her shin against the table as she quickly stands up, her cigarette hanging from her mouth, until she notices Tey glaring at her. "I just lit it; I'll put it out. It's bad for kids to be around, ya know? I really have to quit." She fumbles with her hands and puts out her cigarette, which is clearly half-smoked already, as she dumps it in her glass of water.

"Don't bother." Tey swirls his knife between his knuckles, walking around the kitchen with a look of disgust at the dirty dishes lining the counter and the empty fridge as he pulls the door open. "Go to the grocery store before I decide to stuff your body in the fridge instead."

She was already inching toward the kitchen door when he started walking around, and by the time he closed the fridge, the kitchen door was flopping back and forth.

"I've never seen someone run so fast. Is this a recurring thing?" I state this, gesturing around the kitchen with a frown as I walk over to the baby.

Hell.

I would have helped him stuff Gloria in the fridge. I have an eye for seeing the bullshit and bad in people; she obviously doesn't give a shit about the kids. Maybe it's all for the paycheck for her, but then again, what do I know? This house is probably a lot better than most places; some foster parents shouldn't be allowed near children, much less take care of them.

"Yeah," Tey mutters darkly, his brows furrowed as he stares at me while I gently grab the baby out of her high chair and rock her side to side until her little whimpers quiet down. "That's why I haven't left. If I'm not here looking out for them, who will?"

"I hate this so much. How can anyone ignore this little cute chunkster?" I coo at the baby, smiling as her wide eyes slowly blink as she stares up at me like she's wondering who the hell I am.

Tey groans out loud. My gaze looks up from the baby to see him leaning forward over the counter as he grips the edges until his knuckles are white. He stares at me unnervingly, not even blinking, and it starts to make me nervous. What is going on in his head?

He clears his throat and reaches for the baby bottle sitting next to the sink, checking the temperature while still staring at me. He nods his head to the left, indicating that I should follow him as he walks out of the kitchen. I glance down at the baby with a wary look, wondering if we should make a break for it. Whenever Tey gets quiet and has that special twinkle in his blue eyes, crazy shit is about to go down.

"Tillie, come here. Bring Izzy," Tey calls from somewhere that sounds like the back of the house.

"Izzy. That's such a cute name, cutie pie." I make silly faces at baby Izzy as I follow where I think his voice came from.

The baby doesn't even know I'm sweating bullets over here because Tey hardly ever uses my name. I walk past the living room, where the kids are still playing a video game, and see a dark hallway off to the left. I figure that's where he went. His head peeks out of a doorway near the end of the hall before he disappears. Stopping at the threshold, my gaze bounces around, trying to take everything about Tey's room in at once.

I was expecting medieval torture devices as decor and maybe a naked chick poster here and there... I was way off. His bedding is a blue comforter with a brown nightstand and a lamp next to his left bedside. That's the most normal thing in here.

The walls... Dear God. The walls!

Unicorn and rainbow posters line his walls. He even has a poster of a rainbow with a cat riding on the unicorn's back. It's very, um, Tey.

"I like what you did with the place," I choke out, avoiding looking at the windows at all costs because I'll lose it if I see the pink, glittery curtains up close.

"Thanks, babe. Really makes the place bright, the creme de la creme." His facial expression is so serious that I know he's not joking.

He's lucky I love him and his love for mystical creatures.

"Want me to feed her?" I gesture toward the bottle in his hand, changing the subject before he tries to tell me he's going to be in charge of decorating our future home.

"Naw. Hand her here. I love feeding the lil stinker. She gets this dreamy, peaceful look on her face. Plus, she doesn't know the horrible ways of the world yet. Completely innocent."

My heart cracks open at his words, wondering how old he was when he first learned that life isn't all rainbows and gumdrops. I eye his room more curiously after I hand Izzy over to him, placing myself in his shoes. I think I can appreciate his decorating, trying to keep life bright and silly in his safe space. I'll have to sit the guys down before we find our forever home because they won't get to make one peep over Tey's love for unicorn decorating. I guess I'm going to hand the interior design plans to him if it makes him feel at peace in his own home.

My gaze snaps over to him as he softly sings to the baby, something about a knife and slicing. His black shirt strains against his biceps as he cradles her in his arms, swaying from side to side. I love seeing his dangerous, big hands holding her little head so carefully as she sucks away happily at her bottle while staring up at Tey with a content look. I must have gasped or moaned. I don't fucking know or care. I'm so turned on right now that I'm surprised the wetness pooling between my thighs isn't sliding down my legs.

"You've got a little bit of drool, peaches." Tey smirks knowingly, leaning forward to swipe his thumb over the corner of my mouth.

I would deny it and be embarrassed, but seeing him hold the baby distracts me enough not to care. Sharing his safe space with me while cradling the cute baby with his big bicep and holding her so gently is making me almost dizzy. Seeing him caring for the foster kids and wanting the best for them warms my heart. It also makes my ovaries explode, making my temperature rise with the need to demand Tey put a baby in me. Little Teys running around, causing chaos. They might turn out to be cute little psychos like their daddy, but I wouldn't have it any other way.

"Tey?" I croak out, feeling flushed.

"Yes, precious?" He's glancing down at baby Izzy, but he whips his head up so fast at my next words that I'm afraid he's got whiplash.

"I wonder if our children will have your eyes or mine?" I hum in thought, biting my lip to contain my giggle as he mouths the word *fuck* as he stares at me with wide, excited, bright blue eyes.

"Don't tease me, Tillie," he says so seriously all of a sudden. "I'll put a baby in you so fast, awake or sleeping. My cum is the only thing you'll feel between those juicy thighs until you're pregnant, and then I'll do it all over again for baby number two."

My legs actually tremble, and I feel fucking weak in the knees.

Must. Remember. Now. Is. Not. The. Time. For. Kids.

"Shit." Tey's face is set in stone, his pupils dilating as he storms out of the room with the baby without another word.

I stand there next to his bed, shaking my head to clear it, wondering if I should have followed him.

"I want your panties off and your ankles by your ears. Now. Don't make me repeat myself. You have two seconds to get into position so I can devour this fucking pussy." Tey's voice in my ear makes me jump, choking on a gasp as I spin around to see him standing not even an inch away without the baby.

"W-What happened to Izzy?" I ask with a slight quiver in my voice as I stare at his empty hands.

"She's with Gloria. I threatened Gloria that I'd cut her up in tiny pieces and feed her scraps to the hungry stray dogs around the neighborhood if she didn't take care of the baby," he says with a shrug and then suddenly moves quicker than I can follow. His big hand curls around my throat, making me gasp in surprise. "Do I need to repeat myself, peaches? Believe me when I say you don't want me to because I'll have to edge you for hours by licking this gorgeous pussy," he emphasizes by squeezing my throat hard enough that my breath cuts off.

I flood my underwear, wondering if he'll choke me until I pass out. Will he continue to eat me out even if I'm not conscious? What does that say about me when he squeezes my throat in a rhythm with the opening and closing of his hand, and my pussy matches the beat?

I need more of his crazy.

"Ca-Can you use your knife?" I gulp around his hand, my gaze burning into his as my body shivers in excitement under the pressure he adds with each word out of my mouth.

"Fuck. You know I can't say no to you, my little snicker-doodle." Tey applies pressure with a deep, dark chuckle escaping him, leaning over me as I fall back on his bed with him towering over me.

He stares at me for a second without blinking, his one arm bulging with muscles as he holds his body up over mine while he chokes me out with his other hand. I know he's holding back because out of the corner of my eye, I see his fist near my head clench his bedspread.

"Do it," I rasp out with noticeable excitement and desire.

I can't help grasping his wrist until my fingers are gliding up to his knuckles, encouraging him to squeeze tighter.

"You kill me in the most beautiful way, Tillie." His thumb and index tighten to the point black dots fill my vision, his face fading in and out until I can see his bright blue eyes. "Don't move."

Gasping for breath and coughing with an inhale of air once he lets go of me, I watch him push up until he's kneeling between my spread thighs with a wicked smile curving his perfect, sculpted lips. He reaches into his right boot and pulls out his knife, which reflects the sunlight coming in from his bedroom window. I've seen him polish his knife at the kitchen table for hours and talk to the shiny metal as if it's a person. Even though I asked for this, I can't help gulping loudly as he drags the tip of the blade down the column of my throat as I arch my neck back. I trust him completely, but it's still scary as fuck, yet oddly exhilarating.

Hot.

At this rate, I should stop wearing underwear because they are constantly soaking wet.

I squirm as he draws his knife back and forth, oh so slowly, across my collarbone and down between my breasts. It almost tickles until he nics me on purpose, breaking through my skin and drawing a straight line of blood across my left breast.

"So pretty. I want to mark you so badly it physically hurts not to see my cuts on your skin like a map." He bends down, his blond hair tickling my neck as his long, smooth tongue licks the blood away as I stare up at the ceiling, moaning.

"Shh. You need to be quiet, or I'll stop. It's been my dream to see you in my bed, Sweet Cherry. Don't make a sound." I tilt my head down, my gaze clashing with his as he stares up at me between my breasts with bloody lips.

He licks his bottom lip, skimming over the hoop piercing on the right side of his mouth. My chest heaves, knowing I'm going to be feeling his lip ring and tongue piercing really fucking soon.

"Please," I whisper with a whimper as he places his knife between his teeth. He then crawls backwards on his knees while staring at me the whole time until his thighs brush against my feet.

Without a word, he starts dragging my pants and underwear down my legs until they are tangled at my ankles as my thighs open until my knees are touching the bed covering. I'm spread open like a butterfly and to his hungry gaze as he bites down on his knife until blood starts welling at the corners of his mouth. My legs are already shaking, and he hasn't even put his mouth on my pussy yet.

I'm desperate for him. So wholly and utterly desperate that I'd do anything for him just so I can feel his mouth on me. I watch, transfixed, as he pulls his knife away from his mouth and glides the smooth metal flat up the inside of my thigh. Red starts to seep from a thin line with just the barest hint of pain.

I hiss through my teeth and fist the sheets as I try not to

move a muscle as he circles the tip of his blade on my pelvic bone. He's toying with me. That evil, pleased glint in his eyes says as much, but at least I'm not the only one affected. His pupils are blown so wide that it's almost hard to see the bright ring of blue. I stop breathing altogether as he swirls his knife between his fingers so fast, and the hilt suddenly slides through my wetness over my labia, the handle glistening with my juices seeping out of my pussy. He grins in delight, his gaze staring so intently between my legs as he circles the hilt at my entrance and slowly inserts it half an inch before pulling away. We both watch the handle leave my pussy as he holds it up with a groan, a string of my arousal sticky as it hangs from between my thighs and his knife. His fist grips the curved edge of his blade as blood starts dripping out of the creases of his knuckles and right over my pussy.

"Fuck. Look at this mess, baby." Tey groans deeply in the back of his throat again, his fingers sweeping over my pussy, collecting the wetness between us and smearing it over the handle of the knife as if he's stroking his cock. "You're going to squirt all over my face. In my fucking mouth until I'm almost drowning in you. When I've had my thirst satisfied, I'll spit it into your mouth as you open wide like the good girl you are for me."

He states so filthily, my hips lifting up off the bed for him as a needy noise leaves my mouth. His tone is firm, downright wicked, even as his breathing picks up and his pierced cock bulges in his dark jeans down his thigh. My mouth goes dry, already imagining how the metal balls on either side of his cock are going to feel rubbing against my inner walls in all the right spots.

"Tey. Fucking eat me! I need to feel your tongue deep inside of me—" I stop talking, my words cut off as he spits right on my pussy and slowly, so fucking slow, pushes the handle into me without giving me a warning.

I'm a rambling mess and can hardly think straight as all my thoughts are consumed by him and the pleasure he's about to give me. My breath stalls in the back of my throat as I arch my head back. He twists his knife in a tight grip as his blood mixes with the wetness leaking out of me like a faucet. I can feel the ridges on the handle each time he pulls it slightly out with a twist of his wrist and pushes it back in just as fast. It's painfully slow, drawing out my pleasure to the point tears gather in my eyes. I don't move, knowing he can cut me any moment with just a twitch of my leg, yet my pussy is gripping so tight around the hilt as if to keep it buried deep inside of me.

"You love this, don't you?" he whispers in awe, looking down as he slides the knife in and out.

I can only moan, the sound echoing off his walls before he slides his other hand up my belly, between my breasts, until his hand is gripping around my throat like a permanent necklace.

"Shh. Shh. Naughty Tillie. What did I say?" Tey taunts, ramming the handle into me roughly as I gasp for air. He opens his fist and closes it again before I can even take a deep breath.

My body starts shaking, being that I'm already so close to falling over the edge and soaking his bedsheets. He lets up a little, pulsing his hand on my throat with an open and close of his fist so I can answer him.

"I'll be quiet... but only if you make me," I rasp out faintly with a blissed-out grin spreading over my face as he collars me again, a deep, devious chuckle leaving his sinful mouth.

"Hail fucking Satan for sending me a soul that matches

my own," Tey whispers as he props his elbow between my spread thighs as he pumps the knife fast inside me until we can both hear how wet I am.

His hot breath rushes over my sensitive skin, making me shiver just as his long tongue slides out and the shiny metal at the end of his tongue flicks at my clit at a rapid speed that surprises me.

I would be screaming, but you know, Tey choking me like he might want to kill me.

That's true love.

"Oh, God. Right there. Right there!" I choke out, my voice barely above a whisper the harder he squeezes my throat as tears leak down my cheeks.

When Tey really focuses and puts his attention to something, he's all in. The only sound I can hear is the slurping noises as he laps me as if I'm his last meal. I glance down at my body and gasp as his eyes flick up to mine. His mouth is shiny with my juices while his tongue curls and swirls around the hilt of the knife as it plunges fast in and out of me. He doesn't seem to give a fuck how close his face is to the sharp edges of the knife.

"T-Tey," I whimper as he lets me breathe for a split second before choking me again.

A thin line of blood wells high on his cheekbone as the knife cuts him, and he doesn't fucking let up. My legs start trembling as he increases fucking me with the handle and moving his mouth back up to lightly suck on my clit before pulsing his tongue and starting all over again at a slow pace. Every sensation narrows down to the feel of his plump lips suctioning me, giving little flicks of the tip of his tongue, and breathing hot breaths that make me tremble until his bed is shaking from my body. He keeps doing this before suddenly sucking hard on my swollen, sensitive clit and chuckling darkly as my hips lift off the mattress to ride his face. My stomach clenches as he keeps going from eating me slow to fast every couple of seconds. I can't see as tears continue to fill my eyes at how intense the feelings course through me, my toes curling in pleasure as my legs shake so hard I'm scared I'm accidentally going to move and end up stabbing myself.

"Let go, peaches. Give me all your pleasure because it's fucking mine," Tey mutters against my clit as he flicks his tongue side to side before sucking me back between his wide lips.

He's done edging me. Fucking finally. He looks up at me as I watch his pierced tongue vibrate and swirl around my clit, the lower half of his face is covered in my juices. He doesn't let up even as tears stream down my face or as pressure hits me in the lower stomach, a tightness that has my back arching off the bed just as I start to come. My pussy grips the handle of the knife so tightly he can hardly move it out of me. However, he does at the last second as my orgasm hits me hard.

I choke around his hand as he quickly sits back on his knees between my thighs with his hair falling over his forehead, and we both watch as I squirt all over him. The comforter is soaked beneath my ass, looking like an endless spray while he circles his thumb over and over my clit.

"Fuck. Yes. Just like that. Get me all wet, baby." Tey groans quietly, watching with awe and rapt attention between my shaking legs as my pussy gapes open and closed with more wetness leaking out to soak his shirt and pants.

He releases his hand around my throat just as I felt I was going to pass out. I suck in a deep breath, falling back on the bed in a daze. He ducks down real quick and curls his tongue inside of me with his whole mouth wide open around my whole pussy. I jerk and whimper as he crawls up my body.

With a head nod, he taps my chin and I open my mouth on the silent command once he's hovering over my parted lips. His jaw moves back and forth as if he's swishing something in his mouth just before he spits my cum down my throat. His lips barely touch mine, but it's enough that every drop he collected from my pussy fills my wide-open mouth.

"Holy shit," I rasp once I've swallowed, my whole body won't stop trembling.

"Feel good?" he teases, bringing his knife up to his mouth and sucking the wet handle between his lips until it comes away clean.

"I think you're trying to kill me." I cough, struggling to sit up on my elbows until I can reach his face.

My tongue darts out to lick away the blood from his jaw to the cut on his cheekbone. Copper, a little salty and purely Tey, coats my taste buds. His eyes are closed with a tiny smirk on his lips as I pull away.

"Not today. You'll know when I'm trying to kill you," he says so innocently that I can't tell if he's serious or not.

I mean, I'll take his word for it. If he wanted me dead, I'd be dead. It's as simple as that. I just have to trust him that today won't be the last time I stop breathing.

Maybe tomorrow or the next week, months from now, or years, I just have to live in the moment because I'm never going to look over my shoulder and wonder if I'll die today.

CHAPTER 4

I blow out a bored breath as I tip my chair back onto two legs until I'm staring up at the ceiling, wondering what Tillie is doing right at this moment. Probably fucking one of those fuckers who think they can touch what is mine.

Always been mine. I had been her first.

Well, I wasn't the one who took her virginity. I let the club members do that so she could see I had all the control. She was mine to do with what I wanted. I took her virgin ass, though. That painful reminder will stick with her always, along with the scars as I shoved into her dry asshole. I have dreams of doing it again, over and over, as she cries until her face is a mess with tears and snot. Wrecking and controlling her is what makes me feel alive, and I'll never give that up.

Ever.

"Are you listening to a fucking word I'm saying?"

Ah. Yes. The annoying pitter-patter that never stops nagging in my head. All of these people are useless, like ants that follow the rest of the colony. Their gang turfs and power plays mean nothing to me, but I have an end-game plan that involves Tillie coming to me, and unfortunately, I need these cunts to get what I want.

"What's your name again?" I roll my neck on my shoulders and slam my chair back down until I'm looking at the fucker in his muddy brown eyes.

"Franco," he grits out between his teeth in annoyance as he grips the lapels of his suit jacket and straightens it with a flick of his wrists before crossing his ankle over his knee.

"You're just the muscle around here, right? Why are you at this meeting? Don't you have somewhere else to be?" I draw out slowly as if he's all muscle and no brain just to piss him off.

"Fuck you, you little shit. Do you know who I am?!" Franco starts to turn an ugly shade of red as he stares at me like I give a shit.

News flash, I don't care who the fuck he is. I'll slaughter him like a pig because, in the end, that's all he is. A pig in the pen just waiting to head to the butcher.

"Enough!" Jin barks, his lighter flickering open as he puffs on his cigar until it's lit at the end and circles of smoke escape his mouth.

"I was at a meeting with the mayor. Get to the point: what's so important that you need me here because I have political hands to shake and babies' foreheads to kiss," Franco demands, tapping his fingers on the arm of his chair as he stares Jin down.

Very interesting.

I sense a power play here, and I wonder who's going to make it on the other side. These two don't trust each other. Anyone can tell how they try to keep their facial expressions stoic, except the eyes tell a different story.

Mistrust.

Power hungry.

And my favorite, greed.

These two fuckers are going to be staring down each other's guns at some point, and I can't wait to see how much of a bloodbath it's going to be.

Things just got interesting. Maybe I won't have to kill them; I can watch from the sidelines as they destroy themselves.

"What's so important is that we've been double-crossed." Jin tries to appear calm as if he's not worried, but I see everything.

His stiff shoulders, the way his other hand is clenched on top of his desk, and the firm line of his mouth.

These people worry about their money, drugs, and power. I don't care about any of that. The only thing I want is Tillie. To possess her every waking moment, keep her locked in a tight cage as I use her body over and over again until her eyes become vacant and I'm all she can see. I can't wait to carve my name all over her skin so that in any direction she turns, I'll see my initials deeply engraved on her flesh no matter what.

"Who?" Franco asks tightly as a bead of sweat collects on his temple while he leans forward in his seat.

My gaze snaps down to his hand as his fingers sneak into the waistband of his pants for his gun that's tucked into the right corner.

I bite my lip to keep from smiling as I get comfortable in my chair. Franco looks a tad nervous, which only proves my point that he's sneaking around behind Jin's back. My guess is probably moving money around and planning on taking over the whole operation they have going together.

"My children were spotted leaving Dom's residence by my men," Jin grinds out, his fist gripping his cigar so hard it breaks in half.

Franco scoffs under his breath and relaxes back in his seat.

"I'm not surprised. Nicholas has never fallen in line, has he?" Franco rubs a hand over his mouth, trying to hide his satisfied smirk yet falling miserable.

Jin isn't a fool. His eyes spark in anger, and he sets down his cigar in the ashtray as he gives Franco his full attention.

"It would seem both our children could never fall in line as you say. I have already disowned my children and taken Nicola as leverage for Nicholas to come willingly to me. What will you do to get Logan to obey?" Jin props his feet on his desk and steeples his fingers under his chin while he stares down Franco with a pleased expression.

"No. My son would never disrespect me. He wouldn't... Fuck!" The fool next to me huffs out labored breaths, gripping the arms of his chair until his knuckles are white.

I'm actually having a good time. I was getting bored, however this has taken a pleasant turn of events.

"I would suggest turning Logan to our side or getting rid of him. We don't have time for these, shall we say, hiccups. I want respect. If he stays, I want proven loyalty." Jin stares Franco down, waiting until he gets a silent agreement in return with one single nod.

"Good. I want the girl gone, though. She's a weakness and corrupted our sons." Jin addresses me this time with a raised eyebrow.

I can't help the pleased grin that spreads across my face.

"I have her wrapped around my finger. She won't be a problem." I pat my leather vest pocket, feeling the photo and finger inside.

"She better not," Jin warns me, making me clench my teeth as my finger twitches to reach for my gun.

No one threatens me.

"I'll keep you updated. I have the judge coming over in a couple hours for dinner. Logan and Tillie will be there. I'll have your evidence by tonight where my son stands," Franco announces tightly and stands up, buttoning his suit jacket before striding toward the door.

"Hey, Chief," I sing out just as he opens the door.

His shoulders stiffen further under his fancy suit before he turns around to look at me with narrowed brown eyes.

"Yes?" he grinds out, his left eye twitching as I don't say anything for a minute and take my time reaching into my breast pocket.

"Give this to Tillie, will ya? And please let her know I'll be expecting an answer in two days." I toss the bundled gift with a thin, red ribbon tied around it and watch a look of disgust cross his face as he catches it one-handed out of the air.

He gazes at the photo for a split second and holds it up to the light as he turns the bloody finger around to see the ring that's just past the knuckle.

A signature of the Demon Jokers is engraved on the shiny metal. Only one man ever wore that ring. Tillie will know right away who it belongs to.

"That is all." I feel giddy from the way his whole face flushes red at how I dismiss him.

He'll learn his place. I'm so far out of his reach, that he's just a speck compared to me. I'll kill him without remorse and sleep like a baby, never to think of him again. I wave my fingers at him as my grin slides off my face as he puts my gift away in his pants pocket and a smirk slowly spreads across his mouth.

"I'll make sure she gets it." He sounds like he means more than just my gifts, which has my breathing pick up as rage consumes me, "You know, I get what all the fuss is about. Her tight, pink pussy tastes like pure honey and fucking sunshine as she comes on my tongue... heaven. Gentlemen," he says cockily as he turns and walks away, waving arrogantly over his shoulder.

What. The. Fuck.

"What did he just- he fucked Tillie?" I'm seething and can feel the vein on my forehead throb.

"I wouldn't say he fucked her, more like he devoured her pussy like a starving man. From my understanding, Payne made him when he came to visit, though I don't think Franco put up much of a fight. Don't worry about it, Franco is a man consumed by grief and sees things that aren't really there. Like his dead wife." Jin waves his hand in the air, dismissing the subject before calling his men into the room.

I don't move a muscle. I'm still staring at the doorway and developing a plan.

He touched... tasted her sweet pussy... took something of *mine*.

I was just going to take Tillie once she fell into my arms willingly, but now... I think I'll have to make a brief detour. Kill all the men who have touched her and stared at her naked body. I'll start with Franco. He will regret ever thinking he could taste her honey when it's been mine all along.

My knife will plunge into his chest cavity over and over again until I'm tearing through flesh, tendons, and muscles. Until I can see his rib cage holding his heart. I'll carve my name into the beating organ and rip it out so that's the last thing he sees.

No one takes what's mine away from me. No one threatens me.

I'll end them all, and as I'm staining my hands red with their blood, Tillie won't be able to do anything. I have her right where I want her.

CHAPTER 5

Logan

I stand on Dom's back patio. I take in the tan sandstone under my feet, the glistening pool of saltwater, and the view of the ocean beyond that. There's a wooden arch over my head that covers half the patio with hanging greenery along with blooming bright flowers. A long table and chairs cover the other half of the patio, next to a massive brick fireplace. Bright red and pink flowers with flowing green vines crawl along the walls, through the beams, and leave a sweet, earthly fragrance behind as I take a deep breath.

I won't ever admit it, but Dom has some good taste. It's like the outside world doesn't exist here; it's just an open view of the ocean with gentle waves lapping at the sandy shore. As if we aren't in California, surrounded by crime from all sides the minute you step outside in the front. I like it back here. It's a false sense of belief that everything can be calm as long as you don't turn around.

"It's lovely, yes?" The soft, calm voice behind me catches me by surprise as I watch the figure of a woman stop at my side.

"You have a beautiful home," I grumble, seeking a

glance at Dom's grandma as she sets a tray of iced lemonade and limes floating in the glasses.

"Si. Gracias. My grandbaby has been taking care of me for a long time, even when I begged him not to. A child shouldn't have so many responsibilities at such a young age. When he asked me to move in, I took the guest house to give him privacy since he's a young man who shouldn't have a hovering grandma around all the time. Would you like some sweet limonada?" Isabella gestures to the tray and scoffs as I remain frozen in my spot before she shoves a glass in my hand.

"Thanks," I croak out, sipping the cooling drink, and I'm damn glad I have my sunglasses on so she can't look into my eyes and see how uncomfortable I am.

I don't understand why she's being so nice to me. Unless she doesn't know that Franco killed her son? Jesus.

"My Dom is a lot like you, you know? Both of you are strong-headed, stubborn, and grew up without a loving father." She gazes at me, raising an eyebrow as I sputter on the sip I just took.

"You know?" I rasp, setting my drink down and glaring at the stone squares beneath my feet.

I feel uncomfortable in my own clothing, itchy as if bugs are crawling over my skin. Everything feels too tight. I unloop the buttons of my long white button-up shirt and uncuff the sleeves.

"And I don't blame you. You were just a child with the world on your shoulders," she says, placing her hand on my shoulder with a small pat. "You aren't responsible for another man's actions. Life has dealt you unfair cards, and I'm sorry for that."

My head snaps up, I'm completely speechless.

"I- I'm not sure what to say." I clear my throat, glancing

around, and sigh with relief as Tillie walks out onto the patio from the French doors of the kitchen.

"Nothing to say. Just don't apologize to me unless you are the man who committed unforgivable actions. Also, don't let that one get away. She's a keeper." Isabella pats and kisses my cheek as she stands on her toes while pulling me down to her short height.

She walks away, mumbling something to Tillie about needing to eat more as she passes her. I don't move; I'm still hunched over in disbelief. Is it really that simple? To move on when all you do is feel responsible for everyone, even if you didn't pull the trigger?

"Are you okay, Lo?" Tillie hesitantly asks as she wraps her arms around my neck and smiles at me.

God. She really covers me in sunshine and warmth every time she's around. I soak it up even when I feel I don't deserve her.

"I'm fine, baby girl. Did you have a good day with Tey?" I ask with a shake of my head as I smooth her wild, wind-blown hair back from her forehead with my palm and continue to do so as a blissful grin spreads across her face and her eyes slowly close.

"It was... everything. I met all the kids Tey helps take care of and may have promised to have his children. I think he thought right now, so maybe you guys can talk some sense into him for me before I end up pregnant by next month." She hums under her breath, at peace, as I sway us back and forth while laying my head on top of hers to hide my grin.

If she thinks I can talk sense into Tey, then she honestly doesn't acknowledge that she's jumped off the deep end with him by starting the ball rolling on the baby express.

"Don't let him near any sort of birth control. I wouldn't

be surprised if he starts tracking when you're ovulating. He's always wanted to have children." I chuckle as she groans out loud and places her hands on my chest to look up at me, putting space between us.

"This is all my fault. It's like, I can't say no to him. I want kids one day, but not now. You'll have to talk me off the baby-making ledge." She stares at me with her head tilted and bites her lush bottom lip. "Do you want children one day?"

I can feel my body tense up, and I know she takes it the wrong way when she drops her arms and steps back. I grab her wrists quickly and place them back on my chest, over my pounding heart, so she can't get away.

"I never thought about it, honestly. I'm not sure... if I would be a good father. I haven't had the best role model in that department." I wince, tilting my head up and squinting as the sun blinds me and I blow out a breath. "It scares me too. You talk about me being in your future, and I'm afraid I'll fuck it up one day."

She doesn't say anything for a minute, and I have to glance back down to see her expression because I can't handle the quiet.

"For a man who's so smart, sometimes you're an idiot. Lo..." She takes a deep breath and moves closer until the heat from her body warms me. "You and me, we are forever. I know you'll fuck up in the near future, but so will I. We are in this together."

I bend down and crush my lips against hers, devouring her mouth with every flick of my tongue against hers. I know my grip is bruising her wrist, but I can't let go. I need her always, like I'm sinking in quicksand and she's my only lifeline to pull me free. If she isn't plastered to my side constantly, I start freaking the fuck out and then comes the disturbing thoughts I'm going to lose her. Tilting my head, I take her bottom, plump lip between my teeth with a deep growl as I tug before smoothing my tongue along her bruised lip. She whimpers needily as I pull away, trying to memorize the way her eyes are softly closed and her red lips are still parted and swollen from my kisses.

"Kiss me like that, and you'll never get rid of me," she teases, still a little breathless, as she opens her eyes and smiles.

"Always, baby girl," I promise in a husky voice.

"Also. Fuck Franco. You aren't him. Never were. We will all remind you of that every day. All of us. For what it's worth, and you might not think it now, I know you would make an amazing father," she says tenderly, tugging gently on her wrists until I lighten my hold so she can frame my face between her soft palms.

I haven't let go of her yet. Just a little bit longer.

"Yes," Tey's voice hisses in excitement beside us like a fucking snake, making us both jump from being startled.

"Tey! No!" Tillie groans in defeat as her head rests against my pecs, and Tey slides up behind and rocks them side to side as his arms slide around her waist.

"Oh yes. It's happening. Logan is aboard the baby train, too. Oh fuck! That's how we can get you pregnant, so we don't wonder who the father is. We can line up like a train and impale you on our fat cocks." He shuts up instantly as Nicky appears out of fucking nowhere and smacks the back of Tey's head.

"Bad Tey. You will respect Tillie's wishes and wait to get her pregnant with little Tey's. Although I like the sound of this train idea, you know I'm a top. I like the idea of you fucking our girl while I fuck you." Nicky closes his arms around Tey's upper chest and low on his stomach before he tries to jump us in a tackle hug.

Tey doesn't look upset, though, as he stares at Tillie with darkening eyes and bites his lip, playing with his piercing.

"I'll be a bottom anytime. Need me to bend over? I'm your guy. Have a sudden need to dominate some ass, I'm your fucking guy." Tey chokes on a gasp mixed with a moan as Nicky shuts him up by biting the meaty flesh between his neck and shoulder.

"Shut up. You sound too eager, and that just won't do. When I finally claim your ass, I'm going to edge you for hours until you are shouting to come. That's what you get for teasing me." Nicky doesn't even try to be quiet as he tortures Tey, sending Tillie a wink as she turns around in my arms to watch them and grinds on my dick with her luscious ass.

"That turned you on, baby girl?" I whisper, licking the shell of her ear and nibbling on the sensitive flesh until her head falls back on my shoulder with a lusty moan.

"That's one of my favorite sounds, mama. I have plans for us later tonight to hear what else comes out of that mouth." Dom says this from the open patio doors, taking in the scene of sexual tension with a sly smirk. "Unfortunately, we have other places to be. Nicky, Tey. We'll meet you guys at Dalton's after dinner."

"Why are we heading to the club?" Tillie asks Dom, her voice laced with confusion.

"It's fight night, pet." Nicky smiles slowly against Tey's neck, not taking his gaze off our girl. She can't seem to look away either, as if she's in a trance.

Smooth fucker.

"Fight night?" she finally asks, looking at all of us and tipping her head back to gaze up at me upside down.

"You'll see. Are you ready to go?" I ask, rubbing her arms, loving the difference in how my hands are calloused, and she's soft as silk even over the bumps of her scars.

"Will I ever be ready for this?" She blows out of breath, reluctantly leaving my arms. "Let's get this over with."

That's my girl.

"Don't forget the cooler I set in the trunk for dinner. I took my time making that arrangement, and I hope they like the flowers. Now come give me a kiss, muffin." Tey makes kissy faces at her and taps his cheek while turning his head to the side.

"Let's go." I sigh and put my hands in my pocket as I watch her glide over to Nicky and Tey with a giggle.

She kisses them both on the cheeks, stands on her toes, and whispers something to Nicky that has Tey groaning with a pout.

"I'll make sure," Nicky promises, his finger sliding over her necklace, which he gives a slight tug before it drops back between her breasts.

I nod when he looks at me over her head with a frown as she walks over to Dom and places herself right under his raised arm for her to cuddle into his side as they disappear into the house.

"Don't worry. She'll be safe with us. The tracker is still working." I glance over to the doors again to ensure Tillie can't hear as I question Nicky about the tracking device he put in the necklace.

"I checked it this morning. It's working. I just don't like this. My gut is telling me something isn't right." Nicky takes his arms off Tey and runs a hand through his shoulder-length hair in frustration. "I'm probably just being paranoid. Just check in with me, okay?"

Tey turns and stands beside me with his pointer finger

framing his chin as he looks Nicky up and down with concern.

"What is it?" he asks as my gaze shifts between them. My shoulders are tense as I wait for Nicky to spill whatever is bothering him.

"I don't know. Maybe I'm just stressed; this could all blow up in our faces. We have so much to lose." Nicky stares at Tey, and I think that's the most open expression I've ever seen from him, not hiding behind high walls as he looks at him with love.

"And we'll get through it together. Whatever comes our way, mayhem, murder, or bloodbaths, you have all of us right here by your side," Tey replies back so seriously, all humor gone, and a dark look in his eyes as he mentions murder. As if he dares anyone to come after those he loves.

"For once... I'm not worried. This feels right. It's time our fathers were taken down and Tillie got her revenge. I'll see you guys tonight." I pat Nicky on the shoulder as I move around him and hear Tey just as I head past the patio doors into the kitchen.

"You know what? I'll get my unicorn, and you can use my mouth however we please. Sound good? Oh, and call Nicola and her boyfriend; you know she won't want to miss fight night. I love my bloodthirsty little sister."

Leave it to Tey to think of everything to relieve stress, even when it sounds crazy.

I lied to them both just now, though. I didn't want them worrying even more than they already were. I'm fucking terrified that I'm going to lose one of them through all this chaos we are about to create.

I have to be strong.

The leader.

I protect what's mine, no matter what.

CHAPTER 6

Nicky

I rub the back of my neck and roll my shoulders, hating this feeling of something going wrong. I just want everyone I care about to be within my sight. It's slowly driving me crazy; I feel like thousands of ants are crawling all over my skin every waking hour. I know I'm overthinking, but I can't shut it off. I need control, and it's almost slipping through my fingers like butter.

Breathe in and out. You feel nothing. Control. Control.

My eyes drifted closed at some point as I tipped my head back and let the California sun soak into my pale skin, warming me until my head stopped feeling like it was spinning on my shoulders.

"Come with me," Tey demands in a stern voice he never uses with me, a tinge of worry seeping through, and I hate that he's seeing me this way.

I turn away from the sunshine and look into his blue eyes that draw me in every time; it's like staring into snowflakes falling from a cold winter day with blue skies.

Tey doesn't expect a response; he just grabs my hand to twine our fingers together and pulls me into the house with a determined expression as his sharp jawline tenses. He leads us through the hallways, not saying a word, and stomps into Dom's master suite with a dramatic bang of the door shutting behind us. I can only stare wide-eyed and watch him in astonishment as he paces back and forth like a caged lion. I've never seen him like this.

"Tey?" I ask, clearing my throat as he practically wears a hole in the carpet, and it's like he doesn't hear me. "Tey!"

My shout echoes off the walls, stopping his pacing in the middle of the room to glare at me.

"Shut up. Sit the fuck down," he whispers, even though his tone has a dangerous edge that has me grinding my teeth in anger and turning me on at the same time.

It seems he's forgotten who's in charge of this relationship. I give the orders, and he follows because it's what I need to feel in control. Plus, he loves being submissive, but only for me. No one else.

"You're testing my restraint, Tey. Come here." I exhale through my nose, feeling my shoulders relax as a sense of calm washes over me when he continues to glare but steps closer until the tips of his boots almost touch my shiny black shoes.

"I swear to God, Nicholas, if I see you shutting down one more time and trying to hide it... I'll lose my mind. You aren't alone in this, and you never will be again. If you need an outlet, great, take it out on me, but no hiding. *We* are here for you, so when you feel yourself spiraling, unleash your control on me or Tillie. We can take it. Just don't disappear on us." Tey pokes my chest, emphasising with his point with each word as he shouts in my face.

His chest heaves for a minute as he glares at me, setting my blood on fire.

"Are you done?" I ask, raising an eyebrow.

"Fuck you. And yeah, I'm done." Tey nervously plays

with his metal hoop piercing with the tip of his tongue as I stare stonily at him, knowing he's questioning what my next move will be.

"Good. Now get on your knees, take off your shirt, and unbuckle my belt." My voice comes out smooth, low-pitched with a sharp edge.

It means I'm not fucking messing around, and he knows it as his breath catches in the back of his throat at my demanding tone.

Seconds tick by as we stare at each other until he slowly lowers himself to his knees at my feet while fisting the back of his shirt to pull it over his head in one smooth motion. I look down at him and have never seen a more devastating view. He's fucking perfect, with his chin tipped back, defined veins throbbing on his throat as he swallows hard, as the silence intensifies. He doesn't know what I'll do to him for being a fucking brat. My mouth waters to mark him, to sink my teeth in the fleshy, muscular part of his neck that meets his shoulder. I want to bruise him and let everyone see who he belongs to. Even though my name and Tillie's are on the collar he wears, it's not enough. I want something permanent so that he'll remember me every time he looks in the mirror.

"Do I need to repeat myself?" I ask in a throaty tone, reaching out to trail my thumb over his bottom lip.

"No... sir." He smirks up at me, seeing my pupils blow wide as heat engulfs me with the obedience in that one word.

Sir.

He'll pay for that. He knows what that does to me.

He's being a brat. My hard cock is painfully pressing against my zipper, wanting free so I can fuck his ass until he can't even sit down without grimacing from a burning asshole.

With great care, Tey reaches forward and clasps my belt buckle. Pulling the leather out of the hole painfully slowly and sliding it out of the metal, he starts to grab my pants button, but I stop him with my hand over his before he can get any farther.

"So eager, yet you can't follow my rules. Do you think you deserve an award?" Tey whimpers at the low mummer of my voice, his teeth biting lightly at my thumb before I pull away.

"Punish me. I want you to hurt me. Show me how much you love me." Tey stares up at me with blue eyes turning dark with desire.

He's always had a high pain tolerance, but I'll show him that the kind of pain I inflict is something he'll always remember. It's a good kind of torture that has you begging for more.

"Oh, pet. I do love how desperate you are for my cock. Put your hands up and together," I command, almost daring him to disobey me so I can whip his ass red.

I see the glint in his eyes, the slight hesitation as he raises his arms with his elbows bent, hands together like a prayer, and his fingertips skimming the waistline of my pants. Body practically trembling with anticipation, he watches my every move like a hawk and gasps as I reach for my belt. The quiet swoosh of the leather slipping through the loops of my pants ends with a loud crack when I fold the belt and snap it against my palm.

"Shit." Tey shudders, his thigh muscles straining from his kneeling position.

I don't say anything as I grasp his forearms, running my thumb back and forth over the blue veins running down to his hands. Without looking away from his gaze, I wrap the leather belt around his thick wrists and tighten until I'm pleased enough that he can't escape. Seeing him kneeling at my feet, his blue eyes looking up at me as if I'm someone he wants to worship and pray to, makes my whole body and mind less scattered.

This is my happy place. Right here. Being in charge and yet knowing that I can trust him to tell me to stop if I lose control. He grounds me.

"I'm your god, Tey. The name you're going to chant over and over again. But before I hear you shouting my name, I want you to be a good boy and open your mouth fucking wide so the only thing I hear is the wet gurgle of you choking on my cock as I fuck your throat."

"Oh God," he rasps out, his crystal blue eyes widening as he watches me pull my hard cock out of my pants, fisting myself and slowly stroking up and down until pre cum is leaking out of my tip to coat my fingers.

"Part those pretty lips, now," I demand, groaning as he opens his mouth and sticks his long tongue out, licking up a drop of pre cum before it slides down my length. "Good boy. Keep going. Don't let any go to waste."

Eagerly, he leans forward farther and licks up the curve of my cock from base to tip until he is lapping at all the wet, sticky cream dripping out with hungry noises escaping his throat. My cock throbs, pulsing and leaking at the tip that it almost feels like small aftershocks of an orgasm.

"Suck," I command, my voice deepening as pleasure tingles down my spine from watching him suck me into his wide mouth and hollowing his cheeks. "Oh, fuck."

He winks at me, his gaze not leaving mine as he loosens his jaw more, and I watch my cock start to disappear into his mouth. He wants me to lose control, winking at me with a knowing look.

Fucking brat. I'm going to beat his ass red for thinking he's the one in charge here.

Without warning, I thrust my hips forward and feel my cock slide deeper into his mouth until the tip of my cock is down his throat. He chokes. Eyes wide and watering, he breathes heavily as I reach out and fist locks of his blond hair to hold him still. Counting to five silently, I watch as drool slips down his chin, and he gurgles when I push in more until his nose is grazing my public bone. I release him after counting, let him draw in a deep breath, and pull him by his hair as I slide my hard, thick cock back inside his mouth. I look into his eyes as I fuck his mouth at a slow but rough pace, enjoying every wet, choked noise trying to escape his mouth around my cock.

"You're doing so good, love. I love fucking your throat and feeling you try to swallow around me." My head tips back in pleasure, keeping up the steady pace of leisurely moving in and out of his mouth.

I snap my head back down to look at him when he groans deeply, pausing for a second to feel him swallow before sliding out of his mouth. His chest heaves and tears trail down his cheekbones as saliva strings from my cock to his mouth.

"So pretty," I whisper, releasing my grip on his hair, stroking my fingers over his tears, and bringing them to my mouth to have a taste.

I grunt, loving the taste of him on my tongue. His tears. Skin. Lush lips. Cum. Every part of him, I love, every single part.

"Please," he pleads in a husky voice.

"Please, what? Too much for you, love?" I demand an

answer, wondering if I went too far with him and silently hating myself if I did.

"Let me make you feel good. I want your cum, Nicholas."

Who am I to deny him when he begs so prettily?

"Ask nicely," I command, feeling my pulse with every rough thud of my heart.

Does it make me a sick bastard that I want to fill his mouth until my cum is overflowing between his lips and dripping down his chest? I want to fucking coat him in my essence and smear it into his skin like his own personal lotion that smells of me.

"Use me. Fuck my mouth. Let me suck you off until you're shuddering and bruising my throat so I can't speak for days. Please, Nicholas," he asks roughly, his voice needy and his hot breath making me shiver as he leans closer to put me back in his mouth, but he waits for permission as he stares up at me unblinking.

"Don't swallow. Open." I arch a brow and grip my cock, tapping the tip against his parted lips, and feed my long length, inch by inch, into his mouth as he follows my command.

Fuck.

I love this sight. I love him.

The world could be blown to shit, burning down around us, but I wouldn't notice or, hell, fucking care. Seeing him like this before our deaths would be worth it.

His tongue swirls around the fat tip of my cock, savoring the taste of me like his own personal favorite ice cream cone. He sinks down on me, hollowing his cheeks, and smacks my hand away from the base of my cock so he can glide up and down further each time until his forehead grazes my abs.

"Yes, just like that, Tey. Oh fuck." I groan, willing my heavy-lidded eyes to stay open to watch my cock disappear down his throat and see the hungry way he moves his lips faster in and out of his mouth.

My spine tingles and my abs clutch each time I hear the sloppy, wet noises leaving his mouth. Pleasure fogs my mind, leaving only him and each heaving breath that escapes me the closer I get to coming on his tongue.

"Pull off now and stick your tongue out!" I demand, fisting his hair and tugging his head back as I slide out of his mouth with an audible pop.

He immediately obeys, sticking his long tongue out just as I grip the base of my cock and explode with pulses of cum shooting out of the tip of my cock. Jet after jet of white, sticky cum coats his pierced tongue, and wild, loud-as-hell groans leave my mouth as he looks up at me with wide, burning blue eyes.

Sweat drips down my neck, making the ends of my hair stick to my skin, and trembles of pleasure travel down my spine until I finally stop coming with a shuddering breath. I tip my head back to look at the ceiling for a second to compose myself, exhaling sharply and clenching my fists to gain control of what I'm about to do next.

"Stand up and turn around, love," I quietly say, looking back down to see Tey's eyes crinkled at the corners in a cocky way that won't be there much longer when I'm done with him.

He slowly gets to his feet, drool and cum dripping from his tongue since I haven't told him to swallow. He starts to turn to face the bed, but I halt him by gripping his chin and making him look at me.

"You're going to drop your pants and bend over without a single complaint or smart-ass remark. Am I clear?" I don't hold back, demanding each task, leaving my mouth to be met as I place two fingers on his tongue.

I glide my index and middle fingers back and forth, collecting my cum and coating my digits before I pull away. I nod my head at him, and he closes his mouth, swallowing the taste of me as his eyes slip close with a pleased, hungry hum. He gazes back at me after a second and silently follows my commands without saying a word. The sound of his zipper lowering and his pants dropping to the floor makes my breath pick right back up.

Fucking hell.

My cock is still fucking hard. It hasn't gone down, even though I just came.

I don't see that changing anytime soon as Tey bends over the end of the bed, the muscles in his ass cheeks flexing and thighs straining with barely contained anticipation.

"So eager to please, but that smug smirk is about to wipe off your face after I'm done with you," I say, stroking his left ass cheek and resting my other wet, sticky hand on the bottom of his spine where it meets his crack before, oh, so slowly dragging my finger down between his cheeks.

"Oh God," Tey breathes out, his ass clenching as I rest my fingers around his puckered, gaping hole.

"That's right, love. I'm your god." I chuckle darkly as he swears under his breath, just as I circle my fingers around and around his puckered hole like I have all the time in the world.

I pause and see him start to lift his head to know why I stopped, but he drops right back down with his face turned to the side on the bedding. My palm smacks his left ass cheek, leaving behind a bright red outline of my handprint. It's quite a beautiful display. My hand stings as I connect with his muscled ass again, the sound echoing around the round. It sounds like bliss to me as my eyes slide close for a second, as I stroke his asshole when I bring my palm down on his left cheek again.

"Between you and Tillie, my hands will always be busy. I have a feeling that my two brats are going to need to be punished every day." I smirk as he whimpers into the comforter, his fists gripping the bedding tightly as I glide my hand over his hip bone.

Soft, smooth skin with rugged muscles twitch under my hand as I trace the v of his hip and slide down farther until my palm is wrapped around his hard, long, pierced girthy cock. Cum is dripping out of him like a stream as I circle his asshole with my cum-covered fingers.

"I've wanted to stretch this asshole for years, Tey," I confess, stroking the palm of my hand up and down his cock with a light grip.

"Yes. Please, Nicholas. I'm yours. Every piece of me is yours. I've been preparing myself for you for a long time," Tey whispers, turning his head to look at me over his broad shoulder.

I pause my hand on his cock, tilting my head to the side as I stare at him, and rest my index and middle fingers at his clenching, puckered hole.

"What do you mean preparing?" I ask, spreading my fingers apart to stretch his asshole and coating the outer ring of muscles with my cum before just resting my fingers only fingertip deep.

"Hell, Nicky. I literally got my asshole lasered back in tenth grade, so it's only smooth skin for you. Remember when I was walking like I just spent hours on a horse the second semester of tenth grade? I got my cock pierced and had all the hair removed from my body just for you." He bites on his lip ring while his cheekbones lightly turn pink.

"You did that for me?" I ask, looking down to gather my

thoughts and watch his asshole stretch as I push my fingers in deeper, almost too easily.

"Tey... How else did you prepare for me?" I ask in a throaty voice as I feel my cock jerk in excitement.

"I've known that I'd always be yours since before I even knew what love was. I have waited for you to realize that I will always be here for you and Tillie. I had time on my hands and thought, well, I'd practice with some, um, dildos." The last words come out in a rush, his mouth hanging out with a grunt as I slip my fingers fully into his ass in one thrust.

"You've prepared this ass for my cock one day... Did you know the whole time that I'm completely yours?" My tone comes out adoring, opposite of how hard I'm pounding his ass with my cum-covered fingers and the tight grasp I have on his weeping cock.

"Always. I just waited for you to come around when you were ready." He chokes out on a gasp.

"Such a good boy. Do you deserve an award, you think?" I question as I kneel down on one leg and lightly skim my lips over the red marks of my handprint on his ass.

It's a masterpiece.

He's lost. I lose him as bliss overcomes his expression, his moans growing louder and louder as I pick up the speed of both of my hands. He fucks my fist back, hips thrusting forward as he hangs his head forward with a heavy exhale and moves faster when I rub my fingers inside his ass over the spot that's going to make him see stars. When he doesn't answer me, I open my mouth and bite right over the bright red of his left ass cheek. I shouldn't be surprised, but I was expecting a different response the moment I sank my teeth into him.

Maybe a yelp. Whimpering. Swearing... But who am I kidding? This is Tey.

His asshole clenches my fingers until I can barely feel them. His body shudders and stickiness covers my other hand as cum jerks out of his cock in white ropes that cover the bedding. I stand back up, leaning to the side, to see the mess he made. I'm almost tempted to command him to lick it all up, but seeing his fists closed tightly on the comforter and his arms shaking as he tries to push himself up, I change my mind. Glancing down, I shake my head to clear my head and silently talk to my cock to stay down. I need to give my Tey some love and aftercare.

I smooth my hand up and down his back, watching his shoulder muscles shift with each inhalation and exhalation until his breathing returns to normal and he slowly stands to his full height. Turning back to me, his blue eyes look deep and dark, like the ocean in the moonlight. The blissed-out expression, relaxed smile, and rapid blinking have me smirking.

"Good reward?" I whisper, grabbing the back of his neck and leaning him forward until his forehead rests against mine.

Rolling my head along his, I breathe him in and lightly place my mouth on his plump lips. He kisses me back just as gently, his lips curving at the corner the longer we stand there, not saying anything.

"I think you're right. I'm pretty sure the future holds punishment for Tillie and me. I can see your hand already twitching. Maybe I'll get a tattoo of your handprint on my ass." He sighs again, almost dreamily.

I chuckle and pull away, grabbing his hand and leading him to the bathroom so I can clean us from head to toe while showing him how much I love him with my touch.

"No need, love. Your ass will be red for the rest of your days. I'm pretty sure the outline of the shape of my palm will never fade with how much the two of you get into trouble." I shake my head in exasperation, pretending that it's a huge burden when, in reality, my hand really is twitching to mark him all over again.

"Oh no. How horrible. However, will Tillie and I survive?" he says dramatically, chuckling in delight.

"Brat," I mumble, but I can't contain my grin.

CHAPTER 7

Tillie

I can hear soft jazz music playing the moment we step into Franco's house. It might be French jazz, with a low and husky voice singing. It's the type of music that is meant to create a calming environment for everyone to relax, have wine with friends and family, and make memories with laughter.

It instantly puts me on edge, leaving goosebumps to appear on my arms as soon as the door shuts behind us. The sound of the lock clicking shut makes me jump. I have the strongest urge to run. It's something I can't control; it's as if my body is saying, Fuck this shit. Flee before you end up with a bullet in your forehead.

"Hey. Look at me." Logan's voice is like warm, dripping syrup as he grasps my chin and makes me look up at him. "I won't let anything happen to you."

Protectiveness gleams in his honey eyes, a promise that can go unspoken: I'm safe with him, no matter what.

"I won't let anything bad happen to you either. Both of you," I whisper, straightening my spine as I feel Dom glide up to my side and watch him pull a handkerchief out of his pocket to wipe blood precisely away from his fingers with a pleased grin adorning his face.

"Have fun?" I ask Dom with a raised brow as I look pointedly at his bloody hands.

"Yes. I could always go another round with Franco's men. It's really a shame how easy they are to kill. I stabbed one of the men with a neat plunge to the throat, and the other hired help dropped his gun and ran for the gates without alerting anyone that I was on the property. The security measures make me break out in hives." Dom fakes a shiver and trails his fingers down my back as he guides me into the house.

He does have a point, though. It was stupid easy how he got rid of men roaming the grounds on the property. We pulled in through the gate in Logan's car, and Dom slipped out the back door as the car was still moving. He disappeared into the shadows so easily and took out five men like it was a walk in the park for him.

Logan snorts under his breath and rolls his eyes at Dom just as he passes us. So he takes the lead, and Dom trails behind us. I know they are silently protecting me from all sides, and that alone warms my heart.

I really do have nothing to fear.

The sound of my heels click against the tile floors as we walk past the living room and kitchen. I can hear Diana laughing at something and another male voice I don't recognize. Logan calmly enters the dining room, a step ahead of us, with confidence in the way he gracefully walks with his broad shoulders straight as if everyone else is beneath him.

"Son. Nice of you to join us." I can practically hear Franco's teeth grinding together in anger; we are only five minutes late.

It takes time to kill anyone; he's lucky we haven't arrived

later than we have. He doesn't need to get his panties in a twist; he should know it takes time and patience to eliminate the enemy. I know for a fact that Franco's hands are stained red no matter how hard he scrubs his hands in hot water.

"Logan! You remember Paris's father, Judge Alderson. Have a seat here! We are just waiting on Paris. She seems to be running late, too. Speaking of tardy, have you seen my daughter?" I round the corner just as Diana chokes out the word daughter in a falsely, cheerful tone.

"I wouldn't miss this for the world, Mother," I drawl out slowly, disgust laced in my tone. I can't help it.

She won't ever be my mother. I used to pray for Lorrie to show any type of motherly love for her child, but I stopped dreaming a long time ago. Diana brought me into this cruel world, but she doesn't mean anything else to me. I could probably meet a stranger on a train who would show me kindness, which she has shown me in the short time we've interacted.

She sneers at me, her deep red lips curling, before she straightens her expression into something false, since Judge Alderson clears his throat awkwardly.

"Judge," Logan says in a bored tone as he addresses the balding man next to Diana, "I'm sure Paris will be joining us very soon."

Logan's voice sounds a little too sinister as he drops the cooler on the floor next to his chair by Franco, and it takes a lot of effort to not grin at the inside joke. Diana swallows nervously as her hands flutter in her lap, and Franco's wine sloshes on the table as he places his drink down a little too hard.

"Sit down, now. We were just having a conversation about the new shipment coming in soon. Alderson has pulled some strings and assured me that a few witnesses have come forward and won't be saying anything after all." The double meaning in Franco's voice isn't hard to figure out. Any witnesses who talk will be silenced by any means necessary.

I saunter over next to Logan as he pulls out the chair for me, his lips brushing my temple with affection once I'm seated. I peer across the table at Alderson to see the sour expression crossing his face, his beady eyes behind his glasses glaring at me. I can only imagine Logan touching me in any way that is going to make Alderson angry. He probably has plans for Paris and Logan, wedding bells, and popping out babies just so he can be on Franco's good side.

I wrinkle my nose at him but grin as I trail my hand down Logan's arm once he sits beside me. I want Judge Alderson to know that I'm oh so painfully familiar with the man sitting close enough to me that my hand disappears under the table to grab the hard thigh and climb higher.

Logan doesn't say anything. His expression is stoic, but a glance down shows me the little game I'm playing makes him deliciously hard. I gaze up from under my lashes with a sly smirk at the judge and love how red his face gets in his barely contained rage.

"One moment, Franco. We can't start dinner without my new partner. It's rude to talk about business behind his back. Dom. Please, do join us." Logan's voice comes out bored, as if he's talking about the weather instead of one of his father's rivals.

I peek over my shoulder with a grin as Dom strolls into the room, as if he owns the place, his arms casually clasped behind his back as he surveys the scene in front of him. His eyes are heavy-lidded, slowly drifting his gaze over Diana, Alderson, and, lastly, Franco. If I didn't know him and understood the way he likes to observe people for their weaknesses, I'd almost say he looks entirely unbothered for being a target in a room of people who hate him.

"What the fuck?" Franco shouts, his chair scraping back as he starts to stand and grips a steak knife in his fist. Except Dom puts a stop to a raging Franco by leveling a gun at his forehead.

"Now, now. Is that any way to treat a guest?" Dom clicks his tongue and shakes his head at Franco, like he's a great disappointment for behaving rudely. "Logan. I'm starting to see why you were a complete ass the first time we met, but you've really grown on me. At least you have some manners. Obviously, you must have gotten those from your mother."

"What can I say? Once you start fucking the same girl, you end up finding out you have a lot in common with the enemy." Logan sloshes the red wine glass he stole from Franco and sips it like he doesn't have a care in the world.

I'm impressed. He can act so nonchalant and appear bored while everyone else is practically sweating in their seats. Who will kill who first is going around the table as we all stare at each other with shifting, untrusting eyes.

"I knew when I let you into my house that you would only cause trouble. You couldn't turn out to be anything but a slut. Being raised by bikers only leads to your thighs spreading," Diana directs at me as she pretends to clutch pearls around her neck, her voice laced with disgust.

"You would know, wouldn't you, Diana?" I sneer back at her, flicking my gaze up and down at her as if she's filthy. "I didn't have a choice about who ended up between my legs, but at least I didn't beg for it. Especially when your husband was eating my pussy like he was starving. Funny, I didn't ask for that either."

"How dare you talk to me like that? You're nothing but

an unwanted whore and always will be," Diana screeches like a banshee, her ridiculous blonde hair not moving as she whips her head over to Franco. "Are you going to let her talk to me that way?"

Franco hasn't looked away from Dom the whole time. His forehead is damp with sweat, and his eyes are bloodshot with rage.

"Shut the fuck up, Diana," Franco hisses between his teeth, glancing over at his wife out of the corner of his eye with a warning look to behave or else.

Diana huffs and clenches her fists on the white silk linen covering the table. I shift my gaze to Alderson, who hasn't made a peep since Dom entered the room. He looks like he's seconds away from the grave, his complexion gray and his breathing harsh.

"I no longer recognize you as my son. You're dead to me for being a traitor," Franco says in a low voice, but for some reason he doesn't look so surprised by this outcome; he has pure anger in his eyes.

"You already knew," I state, staring pointedly at Franco as he turns to look at me.

"You were all foolish and naive to think Jin doesn't have eyes and ears everywhere," Franco says smugly, his expression causing a shiver down my spine.

"You are the fool, Franco. My mother doesn't have peace because of you. She's rolling in her grave at the man you've become. She wouldn't recognize you, and I almost lost myself because of you. This whole time you've been blind, letting Jin whisper into your ear like the devil." Logan slams his fist on the table, causing the fine china to rattle as he grabs the rolled-up file out of his suit jacket and throws it in front of Franco on the table.

Franco glances down and back at Logan before slowly

picking up the file, opening it with what I can only describe as apprehension on his face as the blood drains from his cheeks.

"You can't—you have no right to threaten us! I am a judge! I'll have you all thrown in jail, where you'll never see the light of day again." Alderson raises his voice with each threat, but his hands shake on the surface of the dining table, giving away his fear.

"People always think that money will give you power, but that's far from the truth. Don't get me wrong, it's a big part. However the real thing that makes men quake in terror at your presence is not being afraid to do what is necessary to rise to the top. My hands are covered in blood, and my men's hands are covered in blood. They follow me because I'm not scared to get my hands dirty. I must say that Tey has a wonderful way of showing everyone that he is something to fear. For example... Logan?" Dom smirks at Franco but addresses Alderson the whole time before flickering his eyes at Logan with a nod to the cooler.

"Ah. I almost forgot Tey's thank-you gift for hosting dinner. He's sorry he couldn't make it but hopes this center-piece is enough to show how much he regrets not making it." Logan's honeyed eyes darken just like his voice, down-right sinful and with a hint of glee.

It's as if everyone is holding their breath as Logan reaches down and opens the cooler. The moment is suspenseful, especially since no one can see what he's doing. I haven't even seen what Tey has done with his *artwork*. While everyone is watching Logan, Dom strolls around the table on silent feet with his gun still trained on Franco, but he stops right behind Alderson just as the floral arrangement from Tey is placed on the center of the table with a loud bang.

Diana lets out an ear-splitting scream just as Alderson makes a choked sound of horror. My gaze flicks over to Franco, and my eyebrows shoot up as he calmly stares at the centerpiece without blinking, the file crumpled in his fist. His only sign that he's furious is the pulse thudding on his neck and tense shoulders. He suddenly reaches out and slaps Diana with the back of his hand. Her screaming is cut off so suddenly that I can hear Alderson sobbing in his seat.

"Quiet! Or I'll make sure you can't make another noise," Franco threatens in a furious voice, his eyes coolly staring down at Diana. She quickly shuts up and bends her head down until she's staring at her tightly clasped hand in her lap.

"M-my bab-baby girl!" Alderson chokes out behind his sobs and only stays sitting because Dom is holding him down with his hand on the judge's shoulder.

"The world is a better place without Paris. You gotta hand it to Tey, he really has a unique way of expressing his artwork." Logan leans back in his seat, his long legs spread out like a king in his royal court.

My stomach is queasy because Tey really outdid himself by making a statement with Paris's decapitated head. The sight is gruesome yet oddly beautiful. I think I might be losing my mind. Her lips are forever stuck into a stiff smile, her eyes closed as if she's sleeping, and she has a very gray complexion. No one can mistake her for sleeping, though, since, well, she's only a head on a silver platter glued to her perfectly cut neck.

The bullet hole on her forehead is surrounded by a heart of paint, something like face paint you would see at a carnival. It's hard to look away; it's a sight that sends shivers down your spine, but the flowers are so pretty that you can't take your eyes off Paris. The part of her head where the bullet exited left a big, gaping hole, but Tey killed it with flowers.

White roses.

Rebirth and innocence.

It's perfectly ruined by the splashes of dark red blood staining the flowers.

"Are you okay, mama?" Dom asks from across the table, his deep brown eyes looking at me with concern as a few tears drip down my cheek.

"Oh! Yes. It's just... really beautiful in a deadly poetic way. Ya know?" I hastily wipe my tears and grin slightly to let him know I'm okay before gesturing to proceed with the killing.

"I can't wait to tell Tey his art made you cry." Logan chuckles in amusement and reaches for my hand that just wiped away tears, kissing my knuckles before standing up while buttoning his deep blue suit jacket.

"Dom. If you would, please. I'd like to make it to fight night and fuck our girl until she can't walk." Logan nods toward Dom, who grabs a fork off the table over the whimpering judge's shoulder.

Without hesitating, he plunges the fork into Alderson's neck, right over an artery, and pulls it out just as fast. A spray of red gushes out of his neck as he gurgles out a cry, showering Diana like a waterfall with warm blood. She screams again with her eyes squeezed shut and a mouth full of blood. She looks like a scene from the movie *Carrie.* It's only a couple seconds before her screaming stops as she passes out and topples out of her chair, face-planting on the floor out cold. All the while, Dom has his gun still trained on Franco; he makes him watch the judge slowly choke on his own blood. We all watch as Alderson takes his last breath. He slumps forward and dies, his face ending up in a salad.

"Where did you get this file?" Franco asks in a quiet voice, his gaze pinned on Logan with intensity as he holds up the real evidence of his wife's death.

"Your business partner keeps all his dirty work on file. How does it feel to know that you've been shaking hands with the man who killed your wife? My mother!" Logan shouts suddenly as years of rage unleash itself, towering over his father and getting right in his face.

"I didn't know," Franco whispers, staring wide-eyed at Logan. "I didn't know! He murdered my Helen!" Franco yells out with a haunting, grief-filled pain that causes my skin to break out in goosebumps.

I almost, and I mean almost, feel bad for him. Only he deserves this for all the years of hurting his son over and over again. He took an oath to protect and serve but ended up bending and molding into someone evil while turning a blind eye to all the real answers to his pain. He's ruined lives. Killed without remorse to those who didn't deserve it. He made his son hate him and almost made Logan into a villain who would be in so deep that he'd never be able to leave.

"I thought about killing you so many times. You haven't been my father for years. You became a complete stranger to me once Mom died. I want you to suffer. You're going to live with the knowledge that you've been lying in bed with her murderer this whole time. I'm no longer your son," Logan says, his tone harsh and low as his chest heaves.

Franco groans, the sound of pain filled with agony as if he's just finding out his wife died all over again. A broken man sits in his chair, staring up at his son with watery eyes.

"Logan. I'm sorry-," Franco cuts off with a loud gasp as he looks down at his stomach with disbelief on his face.

My chair clatters to the floor as I stand in shock with my hand over my mouth and tears blurring my vision. Logan stands there panting, his right hand dripping blood around the steak knife he's holding in a tight grip.

I hadn't even seen him grab the knife off the dining table. He appears almost manic-looking as he stabs Franco two times in the stomach. His eyes are hard, focused on Franco with pure hatred. I blink rapidly, clearing the tears, and slowly approach him, my heart breaking for him.

"Logan?" I softly whisper, gently placing my hand on his arm and gaining his attention off his slumped-over father who's groaning in pain.

He looks down at me, confused, and his eyes are distant with scrunched brows.

"Tillie," Logan gasps like he can't breathe and draws me into his arms until my cheek is plastered to his suit jacket.

He squeezes tight as if he's afraid to let go, as if he'll drown without me keeping him afloat. I just hold him tighter to let him know I'm here.

"It's okay. You're okay," I say over and over into his neck as I stand on my tiptoes so only he can hear me.

He says nothing except kisses my forehead, drawing in a shuddering breath as he straightens.

"He showed you mercy today, Franco. I personally would love to see you suffer. Be the one to end your life for fucking mine up. You are only alive because he has deemed it. Make no mistake, if you don't bleed out to death and for some stupid, fucking reason to ever show your face again... I won't hesitate to torture you to death." Dom says this with his gun under Franco's chin, so he's looking up at him, seeing the promised threat in his dark eyes.

To emphasize his point, Dom leans forward and places

his fingers on the stab wound, digging his digits into Franco's flesh as he sits there, grunting in agony.

"Son," Franco gasps out and glances over to Logan with pleading eyes.

"You're already dead to me," Logan says in a hollow voice with no emotion as he glances away from his father, whom he once looked up to.

"Let's get out of here." I wrap my arm around his waist, sticking to his side for support as we turn away and start to leave while Dom nods his head to go. He'll follow along shortly, no doubt not done with threatening Franco, but the next words stop me in my tracks with the blood draining from my face.

"Cru-Cruz wants m-me to give you a-a mess-message," Franco says between gasps.

I almost don't twist around. I want to walk out the door and pretend I never heard him. But I can't. No more running.

Logan turns with me, his posture stiff, and suddenly he's the one having to hold me up.

"My pocke-t," Franco stutters out with a cough and weakly pulls out something in his suit jacket with weak hands.

Dom quickly grabs it. His expression is worried, his brown eyes wide as he looks at the object in his grasp before peering over at me.

"What is it this time?" I choke out, my hands gripping Logan's jacket as my heart starts pounding in dread.

"I don't think—" Dom trails off and glances at Logan as they silently communicate over my head.

"Just show me," I demand with a deep exhale and will my hands to stop shaking.

"Maybe this isn't the right time, baby girl. Let's go to the compound and sit down," Logan starts to say, but I glare up at him and lift my chin.

"I'm not weak or a damsel in distress. I can take it. Fucking show me," I demand in a stern voice, not looking away from him until he lets out a sigh and nods toward Dom.

Swinging my gaze over, Dom hesitates and strides over to me with determined steps.

"I don't know what this means, mama, but whatever it is, we'll face it together," Dom promises as he looks down at me with overprotectiveness in his eyes that's slightly tender at the same time.

I hold my hand out, watching his one eye twitch as if he's about to change his mind, except he sees the stubborn expression on my face. He gently places the object in my hand while holding my gaze, and I bite my lip, afraid to look down.

"You're safe. No one will hurt you," Logan whispers in my ear, rubbing my back with soothing strokes.

"Son," Franco whispers pleadingly behind us, his voice weak.

We ignore him as both Dom and Logan walk me out of the kitchen and into the hallway so we don't have to listen to Franco shouting for his son to come back.

Gathering courage, I look down at my palm and blink rapidly, not believing what I'm seeing at first. It's a finger—a male index finger, judging by the size and thickness. I stare in confusion, my heart racing as I try to understand what the message means.

Cruz sent me a finger.

My attention is drawn to the shiny ring still on the digit. I hold it up to the light and feel my hand slacken its grip on the finger in shock.

"Baby girl?" Logan asks in concern, tightening his grip on me as I sway on my feet.

"Do you know who that belongs to?" Dom crouches down to my height as black dots blur my vision.

"Rig," I rasp just before passing out.

CHAPTER 8

Franco

"Son." I reach for my only child, watching him turn his back on me. He doesn't look back as I lay bleeding on the dining room floor.

Everything I knew was a complete lie.

For how long I've known Jin, I figured he would stab me in the back one day, but it seems he's been playing me like a game of chess. That moment, that very moment years ago, outside of Dom's father's house, standing in the pouring rain, Jin appeared out of the shadows like the devil. I shook hands with him and became an ally. I didn't know I was sealing a deal with a man who had killed my Helen. I always wanted to be ahead of others, driven to be better than anyone else. I think back to when I went through the police academy, being at the top of my class, and graduating with Helen cheering for me. She was there for every triumphant moment in my life. Through the good and hard days, when I came home from a long day at work. I supported my family, working to the bone so my wife and son would have a roof over their heads, but Helen used to push me more to see what was right in front of me. She always used to say family is everything, and life goes by so fast that you can miss most of the important moments in the blink of an eye.

I stood by that and tried to make it home for birthdays and holidays, to be there for my little family. That one moment, the second I found out my Helen died... I felt something inside of me collapse. Maybe it was my heart that just stopped that day as I held her one last time, but the drive I used to have, was gone with Helen. I became obsessed with killing her murderer; revenge was my closest friend until I finally pulled the trigger on the man who took my other better half away from me. I didn't see back then that the path would lead me to where I am now.

Somewhere along the line, I lost myself to greed, corruption, and power. My own flesh and blood is a stranger. I have made myself into a man who Logan would never be close to. I am a monster.

"I'm sorry, Helen," I whisper to the chandelier, the bright lights becoming hazier and brighter.

I laugh and cough at the same time, the sound coming out raspy. It's almost ironic. Days ago, I thought of killing my son if he ever betrayed me, and he ended up stabbing me repeatedly instead. I was going to do it too, but Logan beat me to the punch. I can't really blame him for leaving me to suffer with my thoughts as I slowly bleed out. My son would have been rotting next to my wife in the cold, damp soil, and I would have carried on with life and worked beside Jin until I also got rid of him.

My, my, how fast the world does go around.

Helen was right. It only takes one blink, and you end up missing so much in the span of a second.

"Fuck!" I shout, regret burning me from the inside for all I've done, and the bridges I've burned because of my damaged soul.

I already know I won't see my Helen in heaven; my path will take me down to the fiery pits of hell so I can relive this moment over and over.

I

Am.

A.

Fool.

That fucking file. He kept a file on the killing of my wife. Almost like a trophy. I wonder if he would go through the pages every now and then and have a good laugh at my expense. The first page in the file was a faraway picture of Helen, her face turned to the camera, though her eyes were looking in the wrong direction, wholly unaware she was being photographed. A list was the second page of everything my wife did daily: her routine. Pages after pages. Someone, probably one of Jin's triad members, stalked my wife for a long time. Likely, when I started working on the case. It seems Jin has eyes and ears everywhere. He even had paperwork on me right from the beginning of my rookie cop career to the day my Helen died.

The red, bold stamp executed over my wife's smiling photo was like a kick to the gut; the breath knocked right out of you. Or, in my case, a stab to the stomach.

"Oh God. Franco!" Diana shrieks somewhere off to my right, and her blurry, horrified face appears in my line of sight. "You're bleeding! Oh my god! Ambulance." She's muttering to herself as she flutters her hands over me and stands to get to her phone.

"No ambulance," I grit out with a hiss and release my stomach, blood spilling forth from the wound like a river. "Take my phone and look for my doctor. He is on call for emergencies. He'll know what to do."

I dig my phone out of my pocket, handing it shakily to

Diana. She quickly scrolls through my contacts and calls my private doctor just for these emergencies while pressing on my stomach with a grimace on her face.

My eyes blink slowly, closing and opening what feels like hours later, but it's only been a few seconds. I watch Diana through blurry eyes, black dots dancing in my vision. For a split second, her face goes fuzzy around the edges, softer, and I'm staring at my Helen until she's gone once again.

So many regrets.

Death is at my door, knocking very fucking loudly on the other side.

I still have one more thing to do; I'm not ready to meet the devil just yet.

It's the last thing I think before my eyes finally shut, and then... darkness.

CHAPTER 9

Dalton

"Axel," I beckon my club brother over as I wrap my hand with tape and watch him excuse himself from the sweetbutts surrounding him. "Who am I fighting?"

He grins like a little shit and claps my shoulder. "Lug. Godspeed, soldier." Axel chuckles as I clench my teeth together.

"Well, fuck." I finish wrapping up my knuckles and crack my neck while jogging in place. "Watch out for my girl, yeah?" I order as I whip my shirt over my head and throw a few punches in the air as a warm-up.

"Of course, but I highly doubt she'll need it. I have never seen a group of men more pussy whipped than the five of you. She'll be just fine. A queen on a pedestal surrounded by her protective, batshit crazy men. I'd just focus on the fight because you know Lug will rearrange your pretty face." Axel pats my shoulder again and shoves his hands in his jeans pockets while rocking on his heels.

"I don't know why I put up with you, but good to know you think my face is pretty." I laugh as I put him in a head-lock and ruffle his perfect hair. I know for a fact that he takes nearly an hour each morning to style his hair to perfection.

"Not the hair, man! The ladies love these golden locks. Now, go fuck up Lug, so he stops walking around like a cocky fucker," Axel says with a grin and struts away toward his fan club of ladies with a merry whistle.

I can only shake my head and try to focus back on the fight as I shuffle my feet on the gravel of the parking lot. My boots are covered in dirt and dust since they are easier to move around in when I'm fighting Lug.

Why does it have to be Lug of all my club brothers? The guy is a fucking giant with a meat-hammer fist. I wince, already knowing I'm going to be covered in bruises by the end of the night. Shaking my head, I glance around and notice the parking lot is now packed with my brothers in arms, all huddled around rusty bins burning with fire to see into the night as a circle starts to form around the makeshift fighting ring.

It's just a bunch of them standing around in the gravel parking lot at the compound, drinking beers and cheering on with bloodlust for fight night.

Cracking my neck side to side, I walk into the middle of the circle, clapping club members on the shoulders in greeting as they cheer in a chant of my name.

"Dalton."

"Knock his fucking teeth out, Prez."

"Hell's Devils, Prez."

I need this. Fuck. We all need this tonight to blow off some steam. Pops always said that there will always be someone out to get you; see you knocked down off your throne. Sometimes you have to let go every once in a while, or you'll just do the same thing every day until you're six feet under. What did you really live for?

I miss my old man, but I know he's watching over me and drinking a beer as he cheers for me to beat the shit out of someone to let off steam.

I stop at the edge of the makeshift ring, the shadows of the bonfires casting a glow over all of us. We look sinister and dangerous, as if the club belongs in the night. Already, my chest is coated in sweat from the heat of the California night, burning barrels of fire, and my club brothers gathered around in black leather vests as they stomp their feet in anticipation.

"You know the rules. Anything goes, but killing is off the table, gentlemen. Hell's Devils fight with honor and bloodshed!" Axel shouts off to the side with glee at the attention and waits for everyone to shut the fuck up as they cheer loudly. "Our Prez will be fighting none other than Lug! May his big fists not end up killing you, and his monster cock doesn't end up pinning you down in a chokehold."

Everyone laughs as I roll my eyes, yet still grinning until my lips turn down as Lug steps out behind some of the guys and strides cockily into the middle of the circle with his fists in the air. He fucking towers over all of us, huge and stacked with muscles that have muscles until it looks like he'll pop if he flexes.

I'm not a little guy, being over six foot four and having bulging muscles of my own, but goddamn, Lug had to hail from giants in a past life.

I do have speed and focus, something that's been programmed into me at a young age as my pops trained me. I don't charge into a fight. I assess and watch every movement and twitch of my opponent until I know their weaknesses. That's one thing Lug doesn't have. He counts on his weight and charges his headfirst, always without thinking.

I'm not really worried; it's just going to suck when one of

those meat fists knocks into me. Taking a deep inhale until it feels like my lungs will bust, I exhale loudly and look around until I spot her.

My little bitch. Princess.

Logan and Dom are on the other far edge of the crowd, farther back from everyone else, and my club brothers respect them enough to give them breathing room. My brows furrow in puzzlement and worry as I notice Tillie huddled into Dom's side as she grips Logan's fist like a lifeline. She looks pale and dead on her feet, although she still offers me a small smile when she catches me looking at her. It's almost a grimace, and her lip trembles before she bites it. I start over to her with purposeful steps but stop as she shakes her head no and nods over to Lug, who's waiting for the signal to start the fight.

I arch a brow, confused and concerned for my princess. Still, I do as she silently says because she's giving me one nasty glare that kind of impresses me and makes me want to shove my cock into her tight pussy until that blissed-out, tortured expression overcomes her face every time she orgasms. Something's happened, but she doesn't want me to step out of the ring. Maybe she just needs to think, because she'll know I'll demand to know what's wrong with her until she gives in. I'm relentless like that. Especially when I'm worried.

I shake out my fists and try to concentrate on the fight as I look away from my girl. Lug's beady black eyes are narrowed at me as he cracks his knuckles and dances on his feet in a warm-up.

"Let's watch these two pound each other with their fists until blood flows from open wounds and soaks our grounds. Now, hurry the fuck up so I can drown in pussy afterwards. Begin!" Axel shouts, moving out of the way from the middle of the circle as my brothers yell for blood like a pack of animals on the sidelines.

As I predicted, Lug charges headfirst without hesitation and aims low toward my stomach. I brace my feet and tense my muscles as his shoulder collides with my torso, trying to knock me to the ground with his body weight. I'm ready for him, my body absorbing the impact with a grunt as I slide across the asphalt on the balls of my feet.

Without wasting time, I go for his exposed sides with my fists repeatedly and wrap my arms around his waist as we skid to a stop. Muscles straining and sweat already coating every inch of my body, I make sure to have a tight grip on him and lift with a heavy grunt as I tip us backwards. I move at the last second, making sure he is flipped over my shoulder and doesn't land on top of me as I twist to the side while rolling back to my feet. He flies over my shoulder, landing with a thud and a painful exhale. I crack my neck side to side, jogging in place as I wait for him to slowly climb to his feet. He's hunched over and cradling his arm to his side as he glares at me.

"If you call for mercy, I'll happily let you walk away still conscious," I offer, grinning cockily to get a rise out of him and chuckling when someone says '*Oh snap*' from somewhere in the crowd.

Rather than calling it quits, Lug charges forward like an angry bull with a yell. Sometimes, people never really learn from their mistakes, and I'm the one who will show them a different path they can take. It's why I'm the president of Hell's Devils. I'm a leader and will make sure my club brothers will fight more than just with their fists.

Assess.

Think.

Focus.

And for God's sake, stop letting your anger control you.

I hold perfectly still, seeing Lug's eyes fill with glee as he thinks he can take me down, only that hope dies when he's inches away from me. I duck to the side as he swings his right fist, leaving him predictably with which arm he will use. It was almost too easy to avoid and to alternate with a solid left hook to his jaw with a swiftness he didn't see coming. Everyone goes quiet, likely seeing the outcome as Lug's face twists with the punch, and he shakes his head as he stares back at me. However, I'm not sure if he is actually seeing me since he's blinking really hard. It happens in seconds, and I imagine it's like watching the leaning tower of Pisa go down as he sways on his feet until he tips forward. His face kisses the ground, and he doesn't get back up.

"Oh fuck. You really knocked him out cold, Prez!" Axel shouts with a whoop and crouches down to stick his finger under Lug's nose to make sure he's still breathing. "He'll live. Undefeated President of Hell's Devils! Fuck yeah!"

My club brothers step forward, smacking my sweaty back and congratulating me on winning once again. Someone shoves a beer in my hand, the lip hanging loosely from my hand as I swagger over to Lug and crouch down next to him.

"Hey, brother, wake up and have a drink." I smack his cheek a few times, tipping the beer to his mouth as he lets out a pained groan and swallows until the bottle is empty.

"Shit," he grunts and shakes his head as I hold my hand out for him to help him up.

He grasps my palm, and I heave him to his feet while he sways for a second before clapping me on the back with a grunt.

"Good fight, Prez. I'll be sure to mess up your pretty face next time." Lug laughs but grimaces in pain and limps away while our brothers hand him more beers in congratulations for lasting as long as he did in the fight.

"Baby! That was amazing. I knew you would win," a high, whiny voice says to my right just as an arm wraps around my bicep, breasts pressing against my side.

I turn my head and look down with wide eyes as one of the club's sweetbutts, whose name I honestly can't remember, runs her long, pink nails down my sweaty chest.

"Oh hell," I grumble in annoyance, hating when people think they have a right to just touch me when I never asked for it to begin with.

I try to retract my arm, but she's latched herself onto me like a spider monkey.

"Let's go somewhere private, baby. I can congratulate you, and I'll do anything you want. I mean, anything." She blinks her fake, long lashes up at me, not fucking noticing I'm trying to separate from her without causing a scene or accidentally hurting her.

Can't she take the hint that I'm not interested? I lean my head away as she presses closer still, until I can see the clumps of makeup on her eyelashes.

"I'm sure Lug could use some love. Why don't you go find him?" I say, gripping her wrist as she starts to drag her hand down my abs without my permission.

Why do people think they can touch anyone without asking first?

"I don't want Lug. Didn't you hear me, baby? I'll do anything for *you*, even let you fuck my ass," she whines up at me, making my nose scrunch like I smell something bad.

"He doesn't need to fuck your ass when he has mine always open for business for him. He's not interested, so move along," Tillie's voice comes from behind me. Her tone is dark, and it sounds like she's grinding her teeth.

I turn my body, and the sweetbutt moves with me, sticking to my side like gorilla glue, which annoys me to no end.

"You heard her." I bite my lip, stifling my smug laugh at how possessive my little bitch is being.

I tilt my head, taking her in slowly to appreciate what's right in front of me, from her long chocolate hair in waves to her red-painted toenails. Her high heels look deadly but make her smooth, golden legs seem to go on for miles. The sundress she's wearing flutters around her upper, toned thighs. The color of her dress is red and bright, bringing out the light caramel of her skin and making my mouth water to lick every inch of exposed skin. It cinches in at her waist and molds to her perfect fucking tits. If I squint hard enough, I can make out her hard nipples through the material. Well, I could until she crosses her arms and makes my gaze jump up to her eyes to see her glaring at me with her red lips twisted into a scowl.

Well. Fuck. Am I in the doghouse?

I start to take a step to Tillie, completely forgetting about the woman clinging to me like a leech until she's yanking my arm back and rubbing her body against me. Is she humping me?

I snap my head down and to the side in a ludicrous fashion. Does this chick have a death wish? My little bitch is going to mark her territory since the sweetbutt can't take the hint. I can't say I'm upset or anything if Tillie wants to show everyone who belongs to her, but at the same time, I don't want her to get hurt in any way.

"Are you seriously going to let her talk to me like that, Dalton?" Kelly? Stacy? Whatever her name is, she whines up at me and glares back at Tillie while tightening her grip on my arm.

I glance at Tillie, seeing her lips curl in a snarl. I clear my throat because it all comes down to this. I can't fuck up, or I'll probably be punished with no sex for a week.

"Yes." That's all that comes out of my mouth, and I beam at my girl as she rolls her eyes at me before gazing back at the sweetbutt with a menacing step forward.

"If you don't let go of my man, you're really going to regret it," Tillie says in an almost bored tone while inspecting her nails like she doesn't have a care in the world.

Only we all know shit is about to go down when a woman starts taking out her hoop earrings. It goes so silent as everyone pauses to watch Tillie hold her arm out and drop her earrings into Dom's waiting palm.

"Oh, shit," Logan curses, yet wisely rocks back on his heels and doesn't try to stop our girl.

"I'd listen if I were you. I'm not interested. I have her to fill all my needs, and she's all I want," I address the sweet-butt while staring at Tillie the whole time as she kicks off her heels and cracks her neck.

"Not one scratch on you, Mama," Dom threatens and steps back out of swinging distance.

"I'm trying to decide if I should be offended if you think I can't slap a bitch around without getting hurt," Tillie mutters, flipping her hair over her shoulder with an annoyed huff.

"I say a hundred bucks on Prez's old lady."

"You're on. Make that two hundred that she knocks her out in less than a minute."

Whispers from my club brothers reach my ears as everyone watches with bated breath and exchanges money with bets. Not one of them puts money down, with Tillie losing. That makes my chest puff up with pride for my little bitch.

"Oh, please. As if Dalton would ever lower his standards for a skank like you. He needs a real woman, sweetie, and that isn't you." Brittany? Monica? She says with an ignorant smirk while looking Tillie up and down like she's lacking.

"After she's done with you, don't come back. You are no longer welcome at Hell's Devils," I say calmly, trying not to chuckle as the sweetbutt gapes up at me in shock and finally lets me go to screech in outrage as she sets her eyes on Tillie.

"You bitch!" Lucy? Shella? Whatever her name is, she screams at Tillie and lunges to her with fingers curled like claws.

I step back next to Logan, folding my arms as I watch our girl stand still until the last minute. She moves to the side with her leg kicked out to trip the sweetbutt and avoids getting sharp nails gouged into her face. I smirk as Tillie reaches out and grabs a chunk of blonde hair, tugging hard as the sweetbutt goes flying past her. Hoots and hollers rack up the night air as Tillie flings the other woman's head back and literally starts to slap the crap out of her without any emotion.

"She seems tense. What happened?" I comment to Logan, noticing Tillie not letting up, even as the sweetbutt starts to cry.

"Franco is dealt with. Everything went according to plan, but something came up at the last second that none of us saw coming." Logan's voice is strained, like he's in physical pain.

I tear my gaze away just as Tillie starts lecturing the sweetbutt in a stoic voice, opposite how she's bitch slapping the woman around.

"Whatever happened to girl code? I don't fucking understand why you think it's okay to go after a man who's obviously not interested and taken."

I look at Logan's worried face, peeking around him to see Dom watching Tillie's every move with furrowed brows.

"What came up?" I ask, my body going tense as I turn my head when the slapping sounds start turning into crunches of something breaking.

"Cruz has Rig and sent Tillie a gift," Logan's voice comes out strained, tension seeping through his tone and anger.

"Okay, this isn't going to help," I announce and walk into the circle to pull Tillie off the sweetbutt as she starts to swing her arms, fists connecting over and over until the woman under her is sobbing. "That's enough, Tillie."

"Who's the bitch now? Huh?" Tillie yells, kicking her legs as I carry her away with my arm around her waist.

"Damn, killer. Those are some fighting words. Who are we murdering?" Tey appears at my side with a skip in his step as I head toward the club side door.

"Not now, Tey. I'm calling a church meeting with just us," I say loud enough for my club brothers to hear so they know not to disturb us, just as I swing the door open with Tey right behind me.

Logan, Dom, and Nicky follow seconds behind us with hissed whispers being exchanged, except I block them out as Tillie keeps struggling in my grip.

"Put me down, Dalton! I'm not done!" she yells again, gripping my forearm until I can feel the imprint of her nails breaking my skin.

I don't say anything as Tey runs ahead and opens the meeting room with a pained expression. He stares at Tillie when we walk by him. I get it. If our girl is hurting, we are all hurting. Logan must have given them the shortened version like he did with me about what happened at Franco's.

Not giving her a chance to run, I stride to the head of the table and collapse in the chair with her breathing hard in my arms and her long locks of her hair blocking our view of her face from us.

"Take some deep breaths, pet. Watch me; breathe with me." Nicky crouches down next to my chair and gently sweeps her hair out of the way as we see her chest move too fast with each choked inhale.

She's on the verge of a panic attack.

Leaning my head around her shoulder so I can see her face, my breath halts in my chest as I see silent tears cascade down her cheeks. She stares at Nicky, watching his chest move up and down as he takes deep breaths until her exhales are less shaky.

"Talk to us, Tillie. Please," Tey pleads with his fists gripping the chair in front of him, his own eyes watering as he watches our girl stare silently up at him across the table.

"I've had so much taken from me. I keep telling myself I'll be stronger, that I won't cr-cry anymore. But how much can a person take? How much pain? I don't know if I can do this," she rasps, her voice quiet and defeated, making my chest ache.

"You don't see it, do you?" Dom asks, his tone low, as he leans against the table on my other side to look down at Tillie.

"See what?" she asks, looking upside down at him, confused.

"What an incredible woman you are," Logan speaks up, his voice hard and angry but coming from a good place.

"Courageous. Beautiful. Inside and out," Tey chokes out, not looking away from Tillie when she peers over at him.

"Strong. Independent. Stubborn," Nicky states, his voice

deep yet soft as she gazes down at his kneeling position as more tears leave her eyes.

"Sometimes stupid but brave. Sexy. Smart," I say this into her ear, nuzzling the space between her neck and shoulder.

She snorts at that, a hiccup leaving her as she tips her head back to stare up at the ceiling as she swallows hard.

"We'd do anything for you, mama. Fucking anything. You don't have to do this alone. Just lean on us because we aren't going anywhere without you." Dom only speaks the truth, saying what we are all thinking as he places his palm on her head and strokes her hair until her eyes drift closed at the feeling.

She doesn't say anything; she just rests against me with her eyes closed until she stops crying.

"He has Rig. He's baiting me to play a game that only Cruz can win," she eventually says, keeping her head tilted back on my shoulder with her eyes squeezed tightly closed. "Show them, Logan."

My brows scrunch together as I glance over at Logan, my body tensing as he pulls something small out of his jacket pocket and walks to the table to set it down in the middle so it's in plain view for all of us. I feel like we are all holding our breath, wondering what *gift* Cruz has sent to Tillie.

It's a finger.

"Is that-?" Nicky's voice trails off at Dom's nod, confirming whose finger it is.

"Rig. That's his ring," Tillie states in an emotionless voice.

"It's fresh. Probably a few days old," Tey says, moving to pull the chair out and taking a seat while reaching for the finger to examine it.

"Jesus Christ, Tey." Logan pinches his nose and drops heavily into the seat across from him.

Nicky sighs loudly and stands up to walk around the table until he's next to Tey. He grabs a glove from his back pocket and wraps the finger in it before heading to the wastebasket. Nicky throws it away, opens the door, and places it outside in the club bar before closing it again. He strides over to sit next to Tey and collapses into the chair without another word.

"I'm not fucking stupid. I know that sounds bad, but Tillie?" Tey asks, his voice pleading for her to look at him.

She takes a deep breath and opens her eyelids, staring straight at Tey with deep, hurt chocolate eyes.

"I'm not mad, Tey. You're only stating the obvious." She knows how morbid Tey is and how gray he sees the world.

"It means he could be alive, peaches. This gives you a chance to get him back." Tey's voice comes out with so much conviction and hope that I could almost believe that it's possible Rig is still alive even though he's in Cruz's care and missing a finger.

At least it shows that he hasn't been dead this whole time.

"He didn't leave you by choice, Tillie," I grumble softly, tightening my arms around her waist to hold her as close as possible.

"I-I can't think about this right now. Please make me forget. Please," she pleads with a broken whimper, leaving her mouth as she turns her head to bury her face into my neck.

I glance around at my brothers and see the worried expressions directed at our girl. Logan looks away from her while running a hand through his hair with a sigh, and he meets my gaze as I arch a brow at him. He stares for a second longer, seeming to struggle with what to do before he makes up his mind with a sharp gaze over his features.

"Baby girl," Logan addresses Tillie in a demanding tone that right away catches her attention.

She sits up straight, staring at Lo with wide eyes, and shivers in my lap at the command. I love that she's submissive, needing to be told what to do so she can escape everything else that is fucked up.

"Yes?" she asks in a shaky voice, soft and quiet.

"Get up on the table and lay back." Logan smirks at her, crossing his arms over his chest as she squirms on my lap.

"Do as he says," I tell her, placing my hands on her hips to stop her shifting over my dick.

I quickly stand and lift her in my arms as a small inhale of shock leaves her mouth when I place her in the center of the table. She looks around at us with wide, brown eyes and bites her lip as she slowly lowers herself flat on her back.

"Good girl. So quick to follow orders," Nicky drawls in a purr, smirking devilishly when she turns her head to the right to look at him.

"Here's what's going to happen. You're going to take off your underwear and show us that pretty, wet, tight cunt," Logan orders her, his chair squeaking as he leans back in his chair while rubbing his mouth to hide his grin from her as she leans her neck back to look upside down at him.

I stare away from him and take in the view before me. Her tan legs are slightly parted, and the hem of her red dress is pooling around her waist, so I can see her damp underwear. My cock grows harder when the material of her underwear clings to her puffy lower lips as she shifts her hips a little on the table. I groan as she grabs the waistband of her panties and lifts her ass to slide them down her legs. She dangles them on her finger and turns her head to look at Tey just before she flings her underwear at his grinning face. I shake my head as he grips the material and brings it up to his nose with a big sniff.

"How's she smell?" Dom asks in a deep voice, his accent growing thicker.

"Like something I can't wait to taste. Pure sweetness." Tey chuckles in delight at the collective moans of agony from us and pockets her panties with a wink.

"Spread your legs, baby girl, and show us what's ours," Logan demands from behind her, his knuckles gripping the edge of the table as if he's trying to hold himself back.

I feel like I'm dying, starving for her. I place my hands on the table by the outside of her bent knees and bow my head with a deep inhale, practically tasting her on my tongue already.

"And then?" she questions, biting her lip as she peers up at me.

"Ever played Russian roulette?" Tey asks, rubbing his hands together, and then produces his unicorn from god knows where, placing the stuffed animal on the table in clear view of Tillie.

"No," she responds breathlessly as I lean farther down until my shoulders bunch together beneath my leather vest and skim my nose up the soft skin of her left leg.

My eyes roll in the back of my head at the intoxicating smell of jasmine, mint, and slight hints of vanilla from her body lotion. If I didn't sound like such a creep in my own head, I'd sniff her all day like a drug addict.

"One of my favorite games of life and death. Are we doing what I think we're about to do?" Dom's lips twitch as he steeples his hands together on top of the table and watches our girl tremble when I blow hot breaths over the small crease of her knee.

"Yes." Nicky chuckles deeply and leans forward in his seat to grasp Tillie's upper thigh. She's spread out like a butterfly with the sides of her legs flat on the table.

"What are you going to do?" I watch her body break out with goosebumps as she asks that loaded question.

"We are going to see how many orgasms we can get out of you. It might be painful, but you'll come for us. Won't you, baby girl?" Logan raises a brow, almost daring her to say no.

"I'd be careful what comes out of your mouth next, little bitch. Five men to please you; we could do this all day. You have to know we don't back down from a challenge." I love seeing her dark eyes staring down at me between her legs and mouth, hanging open in shock.

This is going to be fun. I'm very competitive.

Tillie

"Yes," I breathe out softly, my chest rising and falling rapidly as I shake with desire on the table.

Everything has felt like a nightmare in the last twenty-four hours up to this point. I'm scared shitless, sad, but over-all... I'm fucking furious.

He has Rig. My dad.

This whole time. I almost wish Rig was dead, that he hasn't had to suffer, and it makes me feel guilty even thinking that. I can't imagine what he's been through in Cruz's care. A regular person would question why Cruz would do something like this. The answer is so obvious that it hurts my stomach. It was just another way for him to torture me and have control over my life.

Ownership.

It all really comes down to that.

I've wasted so much of my short life so far, living in fear of Cruz. I told myself no more. No tears or pain. This time it's different, though. I feel like I'm shaking all over, so angry that if someone handed me a knife, I'd probably go on a rampage to track down Cruz to stab him over and over for each time he's hurt me.

"Any means necessary?" Dom asks, his throaty voice making me shiver and bringing me back to the present.

"Yes. But if she comes before you do, you pass her on to the next guy. I have a feeling we'll all have blue balls since our girl is quick to trigger. The rules of the game are that she comes first, no matter what," Logan explains, bending over my head to trail his lips down my cheek until he ends at my jawline and gently bites down.

I gasp, not sure which sensation to focus on, since Dalton bites my thigh at the same time as Logan. Two sharp stings piece me together, already making my stomach clench in need.

"Hear that? Gotta make our sweet cherry squirt real fast so we can come inside her. I'll be a daddy just yet," Tey mutters in barely contained delight next to me, making me choke on my own spit as he talks to his stuffed unicorn with narrowed eyes, like he's challenging his stuffed animal to argue with his plans.

"No. You aren't coming in her pussy, Tey. You'll cover her breasts instead and rub your cum in her skin so she knows who she belongs to," Nicky commands next to Tey, who sputters and gapes at his unicorn like it's betrayed him.

"It's only a matter of time," Tey mumbles under his breath with a pout as Nicky looks at me and winks.

My chest flushes pink with a blush, wholly flustered and turned on by a wink. God, these guys. I'm hopelessly in love and will do just about anything they say to please them. It's strange. Six months ago, when they told me to get on my knees in the garage, I was fueled with so much anger. I didn't know what to do with the feelings then. But I swear, if one of them said get on your knees at this moment, I'd be in the praying position so fast that my prayers would be answered right away.

"Such a desperate, good girl you are," Logan praises me from above my head, running his fingertips back and forth over my collarbones before sliding them down my dress to the edge of my neckline. "You want these pretty tits sucked, baby girl?" he asks, and a hungry hum leaves his mouth to ghost over my temple and makes me pant embarrassingly loud.

"Put these thick thighs by your head, mama. Dalton is looking hungry, and I think he wants a taste of your sweet pussy," Dom whispers in his smooth accent on my other side, like velvet caressing my skin.

He smacks my inner thigh, my gasp and moan mixing together at the beautiful sting it causes. I obey without thinking, grasping the back of my knees and looking down my stomach at Dalton once my knees are flush with my shoulders almost.

"Daddy's fucking thirsty, little bitch, and this pussy is so wet that I could drink straight from the source and never stop gulping your juices down," Dalton rasps against my stomach as he trails wet, soft kisses from the left to the right of my hip bones.

I jerk on the table at the tickling yet sinful sensation. Nicky taps my hand away from my right knee, holding me open, and replaces his hand there to keep me still. Dom does the same on my other side, his thumb stroking back and forth on my inner thigh enough to drive me crazy with need.

"That's it. God, you're fucking gushing, peaches." Tey groans deeply in his throat, leaning his elbow on the table with his head resting on his fist as his other hand twirls strands of my hair around his fingers while he stares at me without blinking.

"Mmm... You want me to lick you, little bitch?" Dalton mumbles against my skin by my pelvis, dragging his jaw down to rub in small, light circles on my clit.

His short beard feels amazing, making me chase him by lifting my hips off the table as he pulls away a little to wait for my answer. He stares up at my body with deep, violet-hot eyes, and his arm below the table moves in the rhythm, his veins along his forearm making my mouth water. He's stroking his big cock, turned on just as much as me.

"It doesn't matter what she wants. Give it to her until she's crying, Dalt," Logan orders sharply, his voice heavy and raspy as he suddenly jerks the top of my neckline down with a quick yank as my breasts spill free.

I suck in a quick breath, crying out as Logan and Dom each grab my breasts, massaging them with their big, rough hands. I can't stop staring at their tan, strong hands stroking and moving in sync with each other on both of my breasts. Wetness slides down the crack of my ass, pooling beneath me on the table, and Dalton doesn't waste another second. His wet tongue licks me from my ass, all the way up to my clit until he wraps his lips around my tiny bundle of nerves and sucks lightly.

"Oh fuck. Please. Please. Yes. Yes. Oh God, yes!" I cry out loudly as Dalton rolls his tongue around my clit as he sucks, making hungry growls that vibrate along my pussy.

"That's our good girl; you love getting your pussy licked, don't you?" Nicky asks wickedly in my ear as he watches Dalton eat me out like a starving man.

He tightly grips his hand on my leg in warning to not move as my hips buck and gyrate against Dalton's face. I love that man and his tongue, especially as he puts it in my pussy and fucking slurps while lapping at me rapidly.

"Yes. I love feeling your tongue all over my pussy. Please," I whimper as Dom and Logan start tugging on my hard nipples, pinching and rolling between their fingertips.

"Beg harder," Logan demands, smacking my nipples with the side of his palms back and forth until I'm writhing on the table and crying out in need.

"Please make me come. Daddy. Please," I beg softly, biting my lip while my eyes roll back as Dalton groans into my pussy and starts eating me out faster like a man starved, and I'm his last meal.

"Oh, fuck yes. She's going to come all over your face, man," Tey says excitedly next to my temple, his lips trailing kisses down to my ear to tug my earlobe into his mouth. "Soak his face, peaches."

I gaze down at Dalton, his eyes already on me, as if he were waiting for our eyes to lock. He pulls his tongue out of my pussy and quickly sticks his tongue out as drool and my juices coat my clit. Smiling wickedly, he places the tip of his tongue on my clit and moves it back and forth so quickly that I can hardly see it. But I can feel it, low in my stomach and traveling tightly down until my toes curl.

Dom and Logan seem to silently communicate with each other as they switch from pinching and pulling my nipples to slowly massaging until my breasts feel tender and aching in the most delicious way imaginable.

All of a sudden, Dalton stops, panting for breath. I cry out, my body suspended between pain and want.

"No. Please. Please!" I beg wildly, wanting to grab him to push his face back down, but Nicky and Dom stop me by gripping my wrists with a warning look.

"I have to fuck you, little bitch. I'm going to fill you up

with my cum then you're going to come around my big cock, aren't you?" Dalton demands, standing up straight as he drags me closer to the edge of the table to line his monster cock up at my pussy.

"Come inside me. Let me feel it, please, Daddy," I plead with a pained whimper, needing him right the fuck now.

"Shit. Do it, Dalton. She needs it," Logan commands, smacking my breast on the side and grasping my tit harshly before releasing me to do it all over again.

Dalton inhales sharply and plunges into my pussy without going slow. He takes what he wants and doesn't care if I need the time for the stretch. My back bows off the table, and a scream rips from my mouth as my body pushes back and forth with the sharp, loud snaps of his hips as he fucks me roughly. He slides in so easily and out that even as I grip him with my inner walls firm, it becomes a tight squeeze. I'm unbelievably wet that the juices under my ass help my body move onto the glossy table with ease for his brutal movements. I peer down my body, watching Dom and Logan tug at my hard nipples and gaze past their hands as my pussy lips stretch wide and grip Dalton's cock every time he drags his big, thick cock out, only to slide back in just as fast. My legs start shaking, my body moving against Daltons as my pussy squeezes him harder each time he slams into me.

"So fucking tight. This pussy was made for us. Come all over my cock, little bitch. Show Daddy how good it feels," Dalton says, picking up speed and fucking me so hard into the table that it starts to make creaking noises that almost can't be heard over my loud moans.

"Yes, Daddy. Right there. Oh God, right there!" I cry out, looking wildly around at each of my men as they look hungrily down at my body.

"Now, mama. We need to fuck this pussy, make you feel good again and again." Dom's voice sounds harsh, his usual smooth voice rough with desire.

I meet his gaze, and he smirks down at me as my eyes widen when he quickly leans forward and smacks his palm flat right over my clit.

I'm done for.

My pussy squeezes Dalton as I cry out as pleasure consumes my insides, almost sobbing as I shake all over while my hips jerk back and forth in sync with Dalton. Grunts fill my ears, and I hear swearing from each of my men.

"Fuck, yes. You're soaking his cock, kitten," Tey says in a lusty voice, a pleased purr as he watches Dalton's cock slam in and out of my pussy as I squirt in endless streams.

My thighs are wet, Dalton's abs glistening all the way to his big cock with my juices and making me slide easily onto him, thrusting with the puddle under my ass.

I can't look away, my eyes wanting to shut with bliss, but I'm still coming around Dalton, and he's slamming so hard into me with a wild look that I don't want to miss a moment of this. He grabs my hips tightly as he pounds into them fast, his upper lip curling and his thick veins sticking out on his neck and forearms. I feel his cock get bigger inside me, if that's even possible. I swear, I can feel it pulsing.

"Please fill me up, Daddy," I plead with a gasp, more of my juices soaking his abs as they clench when he slightly hunches over my body. He bares his teeth at me, his purple eyes feral as he looks down at me.

"That's my good little bitch. Daddy's going to fill you up with a lot of his cum. Are you ready?" He growls, pumping faster until all I can hear is skin slapping against skin.

"Yes! Please, Daddy. Please," I beg, crying out as I try to catch my breath from this never-ending orgasm.

My eyes roll back, but Logan grips my jaw, tapping his index finger against my skin to get my attention. I pry my lids open, tears streaming down my face, and at this point, I can't even feel my limbs.

"Keep watching, baby girl. Look what you do to him," Logan orders harshly, his voice thick with lust.

Dalton's mouth is slightly parted as he stares up at the ceiling. All of his muscles are straining, and his Adam's apple is bobbing as he swallows harshly until a loud as fuck roar leaves his mouth.

I swear to God, the man's roar just shook my insides, vibrating along the walls of my pussy and making me scream in pleasure.

Thick, heavy spurts of cum hit my inner walls, soaking me so much that each hard slam of his hips makes both of our cum leak out of me every time his cock drags away. I feel it flow out of my pussy until it feels like the table under me is entirely wet. The squelching noise each time he fucks into me is a little embarrassing, but at the same time, I don't want it to stop. It just turns me on more, and I want to keep playing.

I draw in a sharp, raspy breath and lift my hand weakly to stroke his cheek as he stares down at me, breathing heavily.

"I love you," I say. My voice almost sounds dreamily to my own ears, but I don't give a fuck.

I mean every word.

"Oh, shit. You made her cum drunk. Well done." Nicholas chuckles darkly at my side, and I turn my head to look at him with narrowed eyes.

He won't be laughing soon when I'm done with him. I

don't want to stop. I want to feel each of my men and have a blank mind until it's only filled with thoughts of them.

"I love you too," Dalton mutters for my ears only, a long, pleased sigh against my temple with a kiss that's so sweet it makes my eyes water.

I gaze back at him as he pulls away, wincing slightly at the burn and the feeling of cum leaving my body in thick gushes. I smile up at him as he drops heavily into his chair and perches his fist on his chin while leaning back in his seat. His chest still heaves, but he can't seem to look away from my spread legs and the dripping cum leaking out of my pussy.

"That's a pretty sight," he says with a smirk and glances over at Tey with a serious expression. "Okay. I'm on board with baby-making. I kind of want to pound my chest at seeing all my cum covering her pussy. There's so much inside her right now, leaving her gaping hole, that I want to fill her up more." Dalton winks at my startled expression as I lift my head off the table to stare at him like he's lost his damn mind.

"Fuck yes! It's only a matter of time," Tey sings, literally sings, and holds his fist up to bump against Dalton's.

"You aren't putting a baby in me anytime soon," I say, glowering down at his stupid, handsome face as he just smiles at me like I'm adorable or something.

"You don't get a say, pet," Nicky whispers, his tone so bossy and dark that my insides clench at his voice.

"Oh. She likes that. Her pussy is gushing more as she squeezes her insides," Dalton says gleefully and nods his head down between my thighs.

Well. Fuck that. It's my body, and I think Nicky needs a taste of his own medicine. No one tells me what to do, even though it makes my stomach flutter with excitement and burning desire. It gets me unbelievably wet each time. I live for the days to get dominated and bossed around by one of them, almost to the point of being sickening.

I keep eye contact with Nicky as I raise my left leg, spread it completely wide open, and reach down to sweep my fingers near my pussy entrance in all the cum. His eyes darken even more, his black pupils expanding.

"You're playing a dangerous game, mama," Dom says as he holds my leg and bends it farther back until my ankle is almost next to my head.

Logan swears over my head, his hand plucking at my nipple harder between his index and thumb. What can I say? I'm flexible from years of stripping.

"But I want to play, *Papi*. Don't you?" I ask Dom in a husky voice, still staring at Nicky the whole time as I slip my fingers inside myself and gather a lot of cum before pulling my hand away.

"If my queen wants to play, that's what she'll get. Just remember you started this," Dom says it in a tone like dripping honey.

I bring my two fingers up to my mouth, sticking my tongue out and letting the cum drip from my digits until salty flavors fill my taste buds. Nicky is breathing hard, his chest heaving rapidly up and down as he stares at me with a blank face.

"I'm so hard, I'd probably split you in half, fucking into you, peaches," Tey pants on Nicky's other side, his head whipping back and forth at our staring contest like ping pong.

"Naughty, pet. Come here." Nicky's voice comes out guttural as he crooks his two fingers at me.

Feeling giddy and high on bliss, I place my legs down as the guys let go of me and I slowly roll on my knees. Feeling confident and sexy in my own skin, I take my time crawling on my hands and knees across the table to him. It's slippery and wet on the table surface, making it easier to glide my way to Nicky.

"My queen. Absolutely filthy," Dom praises me from behind with a pleased grunt, watching my ass sway back and forth.

I come to a stop in front of Nicky, not saying anything, just staring into his emerald eyes that leave me memorized every single time.

Why does he get to stare at me with those eyes? It's not fair. He has to know how gorgeous he is. Pale moonlight skin, black night sky hair, and green eyes that almost sparkle like jewels.

"I'm waiting, pet," he finally says, his eyes drifting down my body while lightly licking his top lip in hunger.

"Are you mine?" I ask, tilting my head and blinking up at him through my lashes coyly.

"You know I am. Now get over here and sit on my cock before I decide to punish you for being a brat." His lips form into a smirk as he watches a pink blush start at my chest and make its way up to heat my cheeks. "Or maybe I should spank you until you come. Would you like that, Tillie?" he asks, seeing right through me, and scoots his chair back from the table while patting his lap.

I don't stop to think. I fucking obey him without hesitation.

Swinging my legs around, I slide off the table and stand before him as his brother's cum slides down my thighs. I have nothing to be ashamed of; this is love. They're marking me as theirs and showing me that it's okay to break once in a while. They will pick up my pieces every time. It might not fit perfectly together like a puzzle piece, but it's still holding strong in the correct place.

My place is here.

Right along with my guys. I wouldn't want to be anywhere else.

"Nicky?" I say, moving around to his side as I stare down at him.

"Yes, my pretty pet?" he questions, a full smile spreading across his lips until I can see his perfect, white teeth.

God. He really is a shark sometimes, just waiting to strike his prey, which would happen to be me.

"Can you please spank me?" I beg in a raspy, quiet voice, biting my lip to contain my excitement.

"Yeah, I think I just came in my pants. For the love of God, Nicholas. If you don't beat her ass being that she asked so nicely, I won't talk to you for a month," Tey says seriously, reaching out to stroke along my side before squeezing the fleshy part of my hip with a groan.

"You know what to do." Nicky grabs my hand and pulls gently until I'm lowering my stomach over his lap without instructions.

We've been here before, and I'm absolutely wild to feel his hands on my ass again as my body melts into him, my mind silent.

Tey swiftly grabs my ankles and places my legs over his lap, so I'm draped over both of them. My whole body relaxes and breathes easier, knowing the kind of pain I'm about to receive is one that ends in pleasure.

"How many spankings do you deserve, pet?" Nicky asks, gently pushing my hair out of my face and over my shoulders as Tey strokes my legs in small caresses.

The guys are quiet, taking in every moment and word

spoken. It's thrilling—the attention and gazes on my naked body.

I feel powerful this way. It's an addicting type of warmth that radiates the whole body; it's passion, love, and a force to be reckoned with all mixed together that makes you feel like you can take on the entire world.

I'd kill to keep this sensation forever with the five men around me.

CHAPTER 11

I love touching her. Deep, rich tan skin, as if the sun wants to bathe her in its warmth. My palms smooth over her, which brings tingles to my hands every time I feel her beneath me. A sensation of silk gliding along the pads of my fingertips, the rough parts of my callouses, makes her body shiver. I want to bundle her up and tuck her under my neck so I can feel her hot breath on me, knowing she's safe.

Right now, I can't stop obsessing over her legs. I swear they are the most perfect legs I've ever seen. The kind that can wrap around my waist, ankles crossed behind my back to hold on tight. Don't even get me started on her thighs. God. Her thighs are muscular from dancing but thick enough to cushion my hips as I fuck into her tight cunt.

I might be drooling as I watch her wiggle into place over my lap until she's comfortable. She lets out the most content sigh, as if she'd rather never leave this position. It says a lot about our girl. She's a bossy little thing, consistently so strong that I can't help but admire her right from the beginning. I just want her to feel good all the time. I want to be her king, the one who pushes her to go after her dreams but helps her along the way.

For example, right now, she wants to get spanked by Nicky. I'll help her achieve this goal until her ass is a beautiful cherry red. I look at my unicorn and nod with conviction that this can be done. My stuffed animal would agree with me if he would just talk to me, but I only have his facial expression to go off for now. I'm pretty sure he's telling me to fuck her until she forgets her own name and makes her scream mine to the high heavens, where God can eavesdrop on her coming.

"I'll take as many spankings as you think I deserve, sir," Tillie whispers almost shyly, but that tiny tilt of her plump lips tells me otherwise. This girl is desperate to feel Nicky's palm connecting with her fat, fleshy ass.

"Good girl," Nicky breathes, exhaling roughly as if she's sucking all the oxygen out of the room and leaving us gasping for air at the way she demands attention with her beauty without even trying.

She doesn't know the hold she has on us, and that makes me love her even more. She is selfless, smart, blessed to have what she has in her life, and just goddamn beautiful.

"What do you want, darling? Tell us." I lean eagerly in my seat and stroke my hand higher up her leg until it's near the junction of her thighs.

I love staring at the beautiful crease between her ass and thighs; it's the perfect place for biting and leaving a mark. I'd be able to see it if she was wearing a skirt and bent over. Maybe I'll tattoo my teeth marks right there.

Fuck.

I palm my hard cock, putting pressure on the tip and taking a calm breath as I feel it pound beneath my hand. I need to get inside her cunt and coat her pussy walls until my cum plants itself deep inside her. I can't stop picturing her flat belly swollen with my kid or any of my brothers'. It doesn't matter either way. The baby would be ours no matter who the bio dad is. I can just see her cradling her belly, rubbing over the smooth skin of her bump in a protective gesture. My head keeps flashing with an image of a happy home, filled with love and our children. It's all I've ever wanted since I can remember the moment I was old enough to figure out I was abandoned by my parents.

One day.

Maybe that dream won't be so far off because I know our girl wants the same thing. I just have to keep trying until she gives me the green light, then all bets are off. For now, it's baby-making practice, which I'm totally down for. I'll pump so much cum into her, pretending it's taking root until it actually happens, unless... I could make sure she misses her next appointment for her birth control shot. I could easily distract her. She might be mad when she finds out, but it would be worth it.

Hmmm... When is her next doctor's appointment? I need to get Nicky to figure that out by hacking into her phone and finding her OB/GYN office.

"Tey," Nicky mutters next to me, pulling me out of my plans and raising a single brow at me as if he knows what I was thinking: "I want you to fuck her while I spank this perky ass."

I'm already unzipping my pants, lifting my ass off the seat as I grab her legs so she doesn't fall off me, and pulling my jeans halfway down my thighs before he can finish talking. I stare at her thighs squeezed together and can't help myself as I shove my cock between them, fucking her silky smooth thighs with a small rolls of my hips. I spread her pussy lips open, almost coming from the lusty moan she lets out, and watch her gush out her juices just for me.

"Look at you glistening, cupcake. I can see my reflection just staring at this pretty cunt," I mutter in awe and gasp as Nicky grasps my hard cock, stroking his thumb along my piercing with a smug smirk as he lines me up at her entrance.

"On the count of three, fuck her soul out," Nicky orders and rubs the palm of his hand over her luscious ass.

"One," he says, stroking his hand over her right ass cheek so gently and skimming his fingertips over the tip of my cock at the same time.

"Yes, sir." I groan as he presses on the hole on top of my cock and circles his thumb as pre cum leaks out.

"Two," he whispers, voice husky and getting deeper as he stares down at my cock, jerking in excitement at the opening of her cunt.

"Three." His hand disappears as he raises it right over Tillie's ass and pauses to look at me with a slight nod to see if I'm paying attention.

I shove my cock into her with a snap of my hips just as he brings the palm of his hand down. The thud of his smack connecting with her ass is like sweet, sweet music to my ears. She moans, thighs shaking and pussy squeezing and releasing me in a rhythm like a heartbeat.

"Oh fuck!" Tillie shouts, arching her red bottom up higher and changing the angle of my cock as it slides in and out, only to press against her G-spot until she's squealing for us.

Nicky doesn't let up, his palm switching back and forth on each ass cheek until it's blossoming a cherry red of his handprint. We should tattoo that also on her. I love watching her ass jiggle each time I slam my cock deep into her. Those little shrieks escaping from her plush lips drive me crazy.

"This pussy, God, this pussy is gold. I could make a home for my cock right here and stay nice and warm. You'd cock warm me, won't you?" I ask, each exhale and inhale rough as I fuck her faster and harder until she's bouncing her ass back against me to match my thrusts.

"Yes. I love the feel of your cocks inside me. Never want them to leave," she gasps, moaning loudly as I change the pace, sliding nice and deep with each thrust.

"Our slut," Logan praises her, watching with hunger in his gaze as he can't take his eyes away from her big ass.

"Yes. Your slut," she says breathlessly, her voice arching higher and higher as I hit a spot inside that makes her sing to the heavens.

Makes sense.

I am her god, after all.

Nicky reaches under her and plays with her clit, his palm grazing my cock each time it slides out of her wet pussy.

"Right here. Yes, right there," she shrieks and squeezes my cock so hard my eyes roll back as she comes so suddenly.

I pull my cock out, watching her splash out wetness that soaks Nicky's dress pants but push in quickly to feel her orgasm ripple around me. She's so wet, the noises squelch each time I slam into her.

"She came. Ah uh. No more Tey. You know the rules." Nicky tsks under his breath and pulls her away from me as I stand there with a hard, wet cock.

I actually whimper. I'm in fucking pain, and I just want back inside her warm, tight cunt. Nicky places her on the table in front of him and stands to step closer between her legs and doesn't give her any warning just as he slams his cock into her waiting pussy.

"Yes. Please, sir. Please," she begs and leans back on the table on her elbows while watching Nicky's tattooed cock slowly pull out and thrust back in hard that it rattles her breath.

"In a second, pet. We can't let our Tey suffer, can we?" Nicky says, not slowing his pace as he reaches over and grabs my cock in his fist.

He moves his hand up and down, matching his lazy thrusts into Tillie. I tilt my head to the ceiling, pleasure shivering down my spine as I fuck his hand. Tillie's deep moan has my head snapping forward at the sound, and I feel my jaw drop slightly as desire licks at my skin. Nicky has her legs pinned to the table as he smacks her clit rapidly in quick, tiny flicks of his wrists. His back muscles and ass ripple with each thrust. My mouth starts watering as I lean back to get a better view of his tight ass flexing. He suddenly twists his wrist over the tip of my cock and jerks me off in fast movements with the palm of his hand that I can't stop myself as I shout and shoot cum all over his palm and Tillie's pussy.

He lets go, leaning over to kiss my lips with a kiss that I can feel in my balls. Soft, plump lips glide slowly over mine before he pulls away with a smirk and turns his attention back to Tillie. With my cum covering his palm, he places it over her cunt until it covers her from clit to where he's fucking her. It's a white, sticky mess.

"Look at all that cum smeared all over your pussy, Tillie. It's fucking beautiful, a piece of artwork." My chest heaves as I collapse back in my chair and watch just in time as she lets out a high-pitched scream and squirts all over the place in a waterfall. Nicky doesn't make a sound as he comes. He ruts into her until skin slaps against skin, as he grinds his teeth with one final slam of his hips.

"Good, pet. You listen so beautifully. Our good girl," Nicky pants out, grabbing her hips as he pulls out and literally pushes her across the table into Logan's waiting arms.

The table is so fucking wet, she slides in a slippery mess with breathless little moans of pleasure.

"You ready, baby girl?" Logan asks, his eyes accessing her as she nods weakly and wraps her arms weakly around his neck as he stands up and walks to the nearest wall.

He makes sure to angle his body so we can watch his cock slide into her with ease, and our combined cum gushes out of her at the same time. Her back slams forcefully against the wall as Logan fucks her savagely, taking no mercy on her already sore pussy.

"Lo, oh God, I ca-can't," she stutters, locking her legs around his waist yet encouraging him to keep going as she sinks her heels into his ass so he can't stop.

"You can. Feel my cock, how hard you get me. I always want to fuck you night and day. Awake or asleep. Let go and fucking come on my cock, now!" Logan says in a harsh tone, thrusting so hard into her that he literally fucks her up the wall.

"Yes. Yes. Yes. Oh, yes!" Tillie's head smacks against the wall, but she hardly notices it as Logan pounds into her with a force that even impresses me.

We all can't seem to look away as pleasure contours her facial expression, lips twisted but slightly parted as she pants for breath through each rough thrust. Her brown eyes are dark, wide, and almost unfocused as she silently screams. Her neck strains under the pressure as she squirts so much that it looks like it will never end, and it doesn't stop as Logan reaches between them, leaning back to watch.

He rubs her sensitive, swollen clit until there's a puddle on the floor under them.

"Oh yeah. Shit. Shit. Fuck." Logan groans, his picking up speed as he bares his teeth at her before sinking his teeth into her neck to cover his shout as he releases more cum into her abused pussy.

"Any more cum, and her belly is going to expand until she looks full. You might just get your wish, Tey," Dalton jokes, his hands crossed behind his head as he leans back on his throne.

"That's the plan, big daddy," I joke, winking at him as he scrunches his nose in annoyance at calling out his nick-name, which Tillie is only allowed to use.

"Stop being a brat, or you'll be the one with a red ass," Nicky growls in my ear, nipping at my earlobe with a teasing bite, but it still makes me shiver.

"How are you feeling, baby girl?" Logan asks, slowly placing her back down on her feet and holding onto her as she wobbles.

"I'm fine. Just going to need an ice pack after this for my poor vagina." Tillie pouts, but a teasing smile graces her lush, puffy lips. "Now, my king... get over here and fuck me like I'm yours." She crooks her index finger at a smiling Dom, his brown eyes warm as he walks around the table and snakes his fingers into her hair to pull her close.

"Ah, my queen. You are mine. I don't need to fuck you to know that, but I guess I have something to prove to you," he mutters in a thick accent, making me let out a low whistle at the heat in his tone.

"Fuck me like you mean it, *Papi*." She bites her lip and lets out a surprised yelp as Dom releases her hair but only to place his hands on her waist as he crouches slightly at the knees just before he flips her upside down.

Her long hair grazes the floor, and her head is leveled right at Dom's hard cock that is twitching through his slacks. He adjusts her to his liking until her exposed pussy is right in front of his face. He doesn't even break a sweat, looking at ease as he leans his head in and winks at us as he licks up her messy cum covered pussy.

"Well... that's kinky. Didn't know I'd find this hot but I really do," I whisper, biting my knuckle as I stare at Tillie's heart-shaped red ass.

"Fucking show off," Logan grumbles, but he plops his ass against the edge of the table with folded arms over his chest as he watches every detail.

"I'm impressed. Don't know why I haven't thought of doing sixty-nine while standing," Dalton grumbles, a hint of jealousy in his voice for not thinking it first.

"I plan to hang her from the ceiling with ropes holding her whole body hostage. Turning her upside down would be easy, and you can rotate her in any direction. Japanese rope bondage is next on my list to try on our pet," Nicky comments next to me, deep in thought, as he strokes my hair with his long fingers, almost causing me to purr in contentment.

"Hm," Tillie hums, her voice muffled as she bobs her head in front of Dom's lap.

Dom's eyes are closed in bliss as he eats out our girl, deep pleased groans escaping his mouth and traveling into her leaking pussy. The loud, slurping noise and sound of her choking on his cock has me craning my neck to see from a better angle.

Dom lifts his head to take in a deep breath, his lips shiny as he tightens his arms around her lower back to lift her up higher. He catches my gaze and grins as he turns to the left so we can watch her bob her head back and forth on Dom's cock. Her lips suck him off, sealed tight and hungry. Dom dives back in like a man on a mission, his long, broad tongue sinking in deep and lapping quickly at the juices escaping her pink pussy. Her mouth touches the base of his cock as she gags, holding her position before dragging back to take in a deep breath and doing it again. Her lips look fucking fantastic; she loves sucking cock. You can tell by the wicked glint in her gaze, the fluttering of her lashes as Dom groans in pleasure, and her attempts to speed up to please him.

"You taste so good, mama. Like honey on my tongue. Our pussy," Dom mutters between licks, his tongue lapping faster and faster at her cunt with throaty moans.

She wiggles her hips and spreads her legs wider as she moans around his cock. Dom takes those sweet, little pleased sounds leaving her stuffed mouth as a sign she's about to come. He swipes his tongue down and rapidly circles her clit with little, fast flicks until she's creaming his face with squirts of her juices. The whole time she doesn't stop sucking his cock, only doubling down on her efforts and bringing her hand up to wrap around the base of his cock to move in time with her mouth.

Dom throws his head back, cursing in Spanish as he pumps his hips and unloads ropes of creamy white cum into her waiting mouth. He's still trying to catch his breath as he slips out of her mouth and slowly flips her around in his arms until she's plastered to his chest in exhaustion.

"I'm dead. I can't move," she moans weakly, resting her head against Dom's shoulder as she looks around the table at us with a small grin.

Dom collapses in the chair with her in his arms, letting out a groan and closing his eyes.

"We are definitely trying that later." I break the silence

and laugh as she shakes her head in a quick yes before letting out a happy sigh.

"Here, little bitch. I've been keeping some of your stuff around here, just in case." Dalton actually blushes as he holds out a pair of yoga shorts and a baggy white t-shirt.

"Thank you, baby," she says, leaning up to place a kiss on Dalton's grizzly beard before going limp again in Dom's arms. "Help?" She holds the clothes up to Logan with a cute pout that makes me melt.

Will our kids have her pout? I hope so. No one can resist it, not even Logan, as he playfully rolls his eyes and helps her into her clothes without an argument. He looks happy, taking care of her. We all are.

"I won't play into Cruz's games. I won't do anything stupid that will put my life in danger or yours, but Rig can't... He won't last long with Cruz," Tillie says after a while, leaning away from Dom to address us with a grim face.

"We'll figure it out. I just need to find out where he's staying, and then we'll take him down while rescuing Rig." Nicky nods to himself, drumming his fingers on my thigh in deep thought.

A sudden sharp knock at the door makes us all jump, and I rise to answer the door, making sure we are all decent. I swing it open and stumble back in shock as I block the door. Nicky catches me from behind. I never even realized he followed me to answer the door.

"Evan. What the fuck happened?" Nicky stumbles, his voice deadly as he assesses the situation, and I watch his eyes widen in shock.

"A van drove by, not even stopping and dumping him at the gates," Axel grunts as he shoves past us in the doorway and sets him in a chair after looking at the wet table with a head shake.

"Nicola?" Nicky asks in a shaky voice, his throat bobbing with nerves as we wait for Evan to speak.

He's in bad shape. Black and blue bruises with scrapes cover every inch of his exposed skin. I can't even see his eye color; that's how swollen his eyelids are.

"He has her. Sai-said he'll be waiting fo-for a fight," Evan stutters out through cracked, bloody lips, causing his lip to split back open.

"No." Nicky breathes out, stumbling into the door, and shakes his head before running out into the main bar.

"It's a trap. Don't let him go. He'll get himself killed." Tillie gasps, already running after him with fear in her gaze as I catch up with her just as she slams her body into the back entrance.

We shout at Nicky to stop and think, to not do it. Except he's already across the parking lot and heading toward his bike.

Fuck!

Nicky will do anything for his sister, even if he has to trade places with her and sacrifice himself.

Jin

Hours earlier

"It's such a shame, but I knew you would be a failure the moment you were born. I can't even marry you off, for you bring nothing to your family. You are no daughter of mine," I say, cutting into my wagyu steak dinner without looking up at Nicola.

The moment my triad brought her into the deserted restaurant, I glanced up from my noodles with disgust at the display she was making. She sobbed so loudly that I couldn't even enjoy my meal in peace. I said nothing, letting her know my displeasure and making her sweat. The only sound was the occasional noise from my chefs in the kitchen, the shifting of my men around the room, and slurping quietly at the broth of my seaweed miso soup.

The restaurant is right under my office, with the perfect cover, and right under the noses of the FBI. I've had this establishment since my father passed it down to me as a meeting place and cover for the triad. All the books in the restaurant are legit; if you come in with a warrant, you won't find anything. So, to see my daughter in front of me looking uneasy and tears falling down her cheekbones, which she gets from her mother, lets me know that she's terrified. As she should be. No one here will help her here. My triad is and will always be loyal to me.

"Fuck you, asswipe!" Nicola shouts across the table, gripping the table linen as she rises out of her seat, but one of my men steps forward to stop her by shoving her back down.

"Language!" I bark sharply, carefully putting my steak knife down and wiping my mouth with my napkin before giving her my full attention. "Do you think you could betray your family and get away with it?"

She instantly stops fighting the moment my words register, and I nod my triad to step away. She won't be struggling much longer.

"Wh-what?" Her voice comes out choked and desperate, fidgeting with her glass of water before gulping it down with a shaky hand.

"No games, Nicola. It is beneath you and foolish to think I don't have eyes and ears on you and your brother twenty-four-seven," I say this with disgust, barely controlling my anger at the mention of Nicholas.

"What—yeet, skirt, skirt—do you want?" she stutters, struggling with her Tourette's, as she slams her hand down on the table and rattles the dishes.

"That's a loaded question. Do you want to know how I plan to sell you to the lowest bidder in the next auction or how you're just bait for Nicholas?" I calmly tell her, waving my two fingers at one of my men at the kitchen doorway.

He nods and disappears behind the swinging doors into the commotion of the chef's kitchen. I glance back at my daughter, seeing her pale with dread, but her eyes still hold that indifference and rebellion. That won't last much longer.

"Fuck you, old man. I'll never betray my brother." She

lifts her chin and glares at me, but still leans away in her seat when a grin sneaks over my lips in satisfaction.

"It only takes a little encouragement to get one to do anything you want. However, I really don't need you to do anything. This is a lesson for double-crossing me." I reach for my sweet wine and smile into my glass as I look behind my daughter to see my triad guard bringing in the struggling young man through the kitchen doors.

"Let me go! Where is she?" my daughter's boy toy yells, trying to swing his fists, but it harshly yanked back and dragged over to my table.

Nicola gasps and turns quickly in her seat, crying before whipping back around to glance at me in horror.

"Now, don't look at me like that. You did this to yourself. I'm going to send a message to your brother; he'll be joining us in no time." I wave with a gesture to proceed and lean back in my seat, crossing my ankle over my knee to enjoy the show.

It's satisfying to see the panic come over Nicola's face as she tries to jump out of her seat but is instantly stopped before she can take a step forward.

"Evan!" she screams, struggling against the triad guard, holding her back by his arm around her waist.

Weak. She's so weak, it makes me sick.

I sip my wine as the guard holding the boy shoves him to the ground and starts kicking him as he tries to shield his body with his arms over his head. I nod once, and the rest of the six men surrounding us step forward to start beating Nicola's boy toy into the burgundy carpet.

"You monster! I'll kill you!" Nicola screams in outrage, staring at me with hatred-filled eyes that match her brother's.

"Make sure you don't kill him. I want him alive and to be

able to give my son a message." I ignore Nicola, addressing my triad as grunts and the sound of the heel of dress shoes hitting flesh fill the otherwise quiet restaurant.

It's time to show Nicholas what happens when a father disowns you.

It's kill or be killed, but I don't need to worry about that. Nicholas has never been able to beat me.

After tonight, I won't have a son anymore.

A slow grin spreads over my face as I think of the surprise that whore of theirs is going to get. Cruz is going to have fun and play his games with her until her eyes slowly fade and become lifeless. I'll make sure she's used and abused, and then no one will ever want her again.

Worthless whore.

A woman who snared my son into a trap between her legs to betray me.

I'll make sure she's taken on the yacht and shipped overseas to the most dangerous, scary places she's ever been as she's raped over and over again.

I will have my justice and come out on the other side, winning as always, even if my heir is long dead.

No one stands in my way and lives.

No one.

CHAPTER 13

Nicholas

"*N*icholas! Stop! Please stop. You can't go running to him!" Tillie's pleas sound behind me, desperate for me to listen to reason, but I can't for the life of me.

He has my little sister.

Fuck!

I should have been there to protect her! This is all my fault.

I don't stop running, my feet kicking up gravel as I bolt across the parking lot over to my crotch rocket. My chest feels like it's caving in; I can hardly breathe as I swing my leg over my bike and start the engine while flipping up the kick-stand. I ignore the shouting behind me and plant my leg on the ground to swing my bike in a circle with a twist of my wrist to make the engine roar and go forward. I barely make it out of the open-chained gate as Dalton shouts at his club brothers to shut it. Without looking for traffic, I sped out of the lot and hit the road, going a hundred miles per hour in less than twenty seconds.

Not Nicola. I've failed her.

I can't stop that from repeating in my head; the wind is

barely registering as I whip through Los Angeles traffic. I zoom through parked cars on the highway, ignoring their blazing horns, as I drive on the shoulder of the road without a flying fuck.

Getting to Nicola before it's too late is my only worry.

It's almost funny how I know that Jin won't be at any other place but the dojo. It's the only training place he owns since the warehouse is burned down to crisps. He's predictable. I know it's a trap; the practice hall will be packed with his triad. A place where he can try to embarrass me in front of his men while teaching me a lesson at the same time. I've had to endure karate and beatings in the practice hall since the age of five. My fingers touch the screen on the bike, connecting the Bluetooth to my phone, and I pull up tracking for Nicola's phone. The ping of the red dot shows she's exactly where I thought she would be. The dojo.

This ends tonight. Jin has gone too far. No one messes with my baby sister.

I'm not sure how many red lights I sped through or how many near misses of clipping a car with the back tire, but finally I pulled into the street just before Chinatown. A sea of red and bright lights flickers by, people screaming at me as I speed down the street without stopping for anyone. I hop a curb and drive on the sidewalk since a semi is taking up the intersection ahead. Weaving and skimming my leg against the cement to avoid crashing into a little old lady, I run into a street market with a full display of oranges on the sidewalk. I can't stop, not bothering to look back to see the chaos I'm causing. Nicola is all that matters.

Within seconds, I'm pulling up to the dojo and jumping off my bike without even parking it. I hear it crash somewhere behind me as I run into the three-story building in front of me. Shoving my shoulder into the front glass doors, I skid into the lobby and found it completely empty. It's not a surprise. Jin doesn't see me as a threat. I jog over to the stairwell and start taking the steps two at a time without pausing. The only sound is my deep breathing and the echo of my shoes as I run up to the third floor. Swinging the door open, I step into the dojo on soft mats to muffle the sound of my steps. I'm not surprised to see the triad lining the walls, each dressed in black suits and not saying a word. My gaze quickly shifts to the middle of the room, seeing Jin standing on the mat with an expression void of emotion, just like his dead eyes.

"Weak," Jin says in a booming voice, his gaze searching the room and looking at each triad member before looking back at me. "Nicholas is an example of weakness, the definition. He came running even though he had to know it was a trap, all for the love he carries for his sister. He let his heart carry him to his own death."

I try to keep my expression neutral, almost bored, but at the moment Jin turns his back on me and strides forward to reveal Nicola between two of the goons... I lose my cool. I see bruises on her porcelain skin, the cut still bleeding on her trembling lip and shaking limbs.

"She's your own flesh and blood! How dare you lay a hand on her! You will pay for that!" I'm screaming—beyond furious.

I don't remember swiftly walking across the mats, intending to kill Jin where he stands next to my sister. But I'm stopped by his goons laying their palms on my shoulders and pushing me back even as I struggle against them.

"Rash and that temper. Such a disappointment. You are no son of mine," Jin drawls, shaking his head at me in disgust as he starts circling the room like a shark in the water. "Let him go. He'll finally learn where he belongs once I'm done with him. Under my heel, before I kill him," he tells his triad members, holding me back with a nod of his head.

They slowly release me, and I shake out my arms, looking at my cuff links as I unbutton them to roll my sleeves up so I can try to calm down. I can't look at Nicola again. Seeing her beaten makes all rational thoughts vanish. I need to focus to end this. I glance up after taking a slow breath that's barely noticeable, my gaze connecting with Jin as he finishes circling the room to come to a stop a few meters away from me.

"I was never your son, Jin. Carrying on your name would be a disgrace to mankind. I will never be like you, and the next time I see you, I'll be burying the heels of my shoes into your graveyard dirt." I square my shoulders and don't look away from him as his face turns red in rage.

"I'll cut out your tongue for that while keeping you alive long enough to see your sister and friends die." His lips curl at the edges as he nods behind me, just as I hear shocked gasps and yelling coming from the stairwell doorway.

I don't look. I can't get distracted, even as my skin itches to protect my brothers and Tillie. I can hear a struggle behind me, grunts and growls of outrage as the triad holds them back. They shouldn't have come. I have no other option but to win, no matter what, against Jin. By any means necessary.

"And the girl. She will sell for a high price. That cunt won't be tight for long," Jin taunts and flickers his gaze quickly back to me when my hands twitch at my sides.

He notices everything. Always has. It's why I have to be one step ahead of him.

"Does that bug you, Nicholas? Knowing she will be used

over and over again by brute men, stuffed full of cocks before she eventually dies on a seedy little cot dried with her blood and cum." Jin tilts his head at me, his jaw ticking when I don't show any emotion, even though I'm boiling alive inside at each word coming out of his vile mouth.

He sighs in disappointment and whips a gun out of his waistband, pointing the barrel at my forehead, inches away.

"Simply a waste," he says, his finger starting to press on the trigger as I keep my eyes locked on his without blinking.

"No! You son of a bitch!" Nicola screams somewhere behind Jin as she struggles.

"Don't do this! Please! Please!" Tillie shouts with pleas that fall on deaf ears.

I ignore everything: grunts, skin smacking skin, and screams. All that matters is showing Jin that he can never win.

"A gun? How original," I say, in a bored tone, even though my mind is racing with how to get everyone I love out safely. "I figured a man in power such as yourself wouldn't resort to a gun when he can kill with his bare hands. It's almost-" I trail off, hiding a smirk as Jin's eyes narrow as he processes my every word.

"Almost, what?" he grits through his teeth, agitated and furious that I'm not showing fear.

"Pathetic, really," I finish and know I have him as he lowers his gun and peers around at his triad members, who stare warily at him but hold no respect.

Triads don't need to resort to weapons when we can kill a man with our bare hands. It's something we were all taught from the very beginning—to prove to ourselves that we are strong and deserve a place in the triad. Jin is going against everything he has always preached and the lessons he has demanded of his members to make them unstoppable in any situation. To use a gun in front of his men while I stand here unafraid and challenge him only shows he shouldn't be in charge if he doesn't believe his own beliefs.

"How dare you? When I'm done with you, wiping your face into the mats stained with your blood, you'll know before your last breath that you couldn't save any of them," Jin threatens, his eyes narrowed in hatred as he lowers the gun and hands it over to one of his goons before stepping back.

He unbuttons his shirt, handing the garment to a waiting hand once removed, as he shifts his head back and forth, cracking his neck before dropping into a direct bridge of kung fu. I don't bother to strip off any article of clothing; I don't need to parade around my strength for it to be seen. Each taekwondo pose will define every movement, with or without a shirt. I glare at Jin, moving my right foot back with my right fist tucked into my side into an outside block pose. With my elbow tight against my side, I lean forward and crook my finger at him in a challenge that I know will piss him off.

I don't know who moves first, but I'm dodging an axel kick that's aiming right at my head. I duck down low into a crouch at the last second to sweep out his feet beneath him. Spinning in a circle on one leg, I grunt as I jump to my feet as he steps away before I can make contact to lay him flat out. The blow to the ribs hardly fazes me. I absorb the pain and stop the next punch with a hand knife low block while retaliating by jabbing my fist into his gut two times. He hooks his forearm around my waist and tries to knock me onto the mat, but I can't let him do that. I won't ever be able to get back up if he pins me down.

It goes on for minutes that feel like hours until my white

shirt sticks to me like a second coat of skin from sweat. Jin jumps back, rapidly breathing as he bounces on the balls of his feet with a red face. Either from anger or a lack of oxygen.

"You want to know the difference between me and you?" I ask, exhaling slowly to expand my chest and breathe properly.

He doesn't answer; he just yells and grunts as he suddenly races forward with one palm extended toward my face and draws his other hand back in distraction. I avoid the lethal movement, knowing he really would kill me if the heel of his palm connected under my nose. I would have bled out from my brain, shutting down and drowning in blood.

"I'd fight for the people I love, not stopping even when I could barely move my battered body. That is what is different between us, Jin. You only care about *yourself*. No one would ever keep fighting for you or miss you. You'll die here tonight knowing that," I snarl out, meaning every damn word coming out of my mouth like a promise.

One of us isn't leaving this room tonight.

"Kick his ass, Nicky! Go fuck yourself, you waffle twat! Just die already, Jin!" Nicola cheers in the background, distracting me for a split second when I hear a thud and a moan of agony.

Turning to the left, I realize my mistake as Tillie screams louder than I've ever heard. It's haunting, a sound, a devastation.

It only takes a second for things to change—one moment that can either go down two different paths or split within a road. Good or bad.

I think I just went down the wrong path.

CHAPTER 14

Tillie

My heart hasn't stopped racing since Nicky went tearing out of the club, a man possessed to protect his sister. I honestly don't remember the ride over to the dojo. I just remember telling Dom to drive faster and practically yelling at Tey to tell me where Nicky could be heading. He didn't even stop for one second to talk to us; he ran so fast, like hellhounds were on his heels. Luckily, Evan was insightful on where exactly Nicola is being held captive.

Poor Evan. God. He looked like absolute shit. But the club brothers will get him patched up and cared for. I promised him just before hopping in the car that I'd keep him updated once Nicola was back with us. He seemed so lost and in deep pain inside and out. I'll make sure that he'll have his girlfriend safely back in his arms.

I gripped Dom's shoulder from the backseat the whole drive to Chinatown, the longest ride of twenty minutes. I can't lose Nicola. She's like a sister to me, one I never knew I was missing in my life. Ride or die, bitch. My whole body is trembling as we squeal on spinning tires into an empty parking lot in front of a massive, three-story building. My hand is already on the door handle, but Dom stops me before I can jump out of the car.

"We stick together, and we don't do anything fucking stupid." Dom twists in his seat so he can stare at all of us before his gaze lands on me and lingers. "If shit hits the fan, I'm not taking any risks when it comes to you, mama."

I gulp as his intense dark eyes pierce my own, not letting me go until I nod in agreement, even though I'm lying. I'll just do just about anything to make sure my men are not in harm's way and bestie Nicola.

"Say it," Logan growls in the passenger seat, glaring at me like he knows what I'm thinking.

"I'll be careful," I reply, staring him down until he finally looks away with a clenched jaw.

Tey shifts in his seat next to me, practically vibrating with energy, and I know he's worried. I wonder if he's also picking up on this doomed feeling as I am. As if time is limited and it's all going to come crashing down.

"Let's fucking do this. Guns loaded," Dalton thunders in a deep voice, bouncing off the clothed car ceiling and vibrating in my ears.

All the doors open as we climb out, and I feel my throat go dry as the guys check their guns before putting the weapons away in their waistbands.

Why is that look of determination on their faces sexy? Fuck me, I'm a mess. Now is not the time. I twist away and catch Tey's gaze as he flips his knife between his fingers, winking at me while blowing an air kiss. I roll my eyes as I roughly pull the front entrance door open and try to focus as the guys form a protective circle around me while heading toward the stairway off to the left.

Our feet pound up the stairs, where we hear voices—

Logan and Dom leading the way. They enter in a rush and stop in the doorway, so I have to shove my way between their broad shoulders to see what's happening. I quickly take in my surroundings, meeting Nicola's gaze across the room with relief that she's here and alive. She looks fucking pissed, though, wiggling between the two goons on her sides holding her in place. My eyes snap right to the middle of the room, and I find Jin looking at me with disgust and a hint of glee.

His words start to register as he taunts Nicky. I begin to walk over to Nicky, but I'm immediately stopped by the triad that encircles around us. One goon lays a bruising grip on my arm, and the guys go nuts by shoving the idiot who dared to touch me. I'm shoved back behind Dom and can hear Jin screaming in a haunting voice that gives me chills as the guys try to fight their way toward Nicky. Jin's trying to get a rise out of his son, wanting him to lose control, but he won't get anywhere. Nicky always wears a cool, calm mask. Always. Standing on my toes, I peer over Dom's shoulder to see Jin pull a gun out and aim the barrel between Nicky's eyes.

I hear screaming, sounding terrified, and realize it's me as I beg Jin not to do this. I'll stoop to any level if I have to; I'd rather do that than see one of the men I love shot to death. Nicky doesn't even flinch at the weapon aimed at him. He stands straight and has a stoic expression. Challenging. Fucking daring.

He's beautiful.

I stop struggling and hold my breath as Jin puts the gun away. One second, they are staring each other down, and the next, they are fighting with their whole bodies in a blur. I've never seen karate; the movements are fascinating—a deadly beauty you can't look away from.

You literally put your whole body behind every movement.

I cringe as skin smacks harshly against flesh, praying that Nicky will be okay. He'll be bruised, but I know he'll make it out on the other side. He's determined, and he has people who love him and are waiting for him.

Almost in slow motion, everything ceases to exist as Nicky gets distracted when one of the triads backhands Nicola across the face. She moans in pain and shakes her head while spitting blood up on the floor at his feet with a sneer. I blink, and suddenly, Nicky isn't standing where he was a second ago. He's halfway across the mats on his side, lying down, clenching his ribs as Jin lowers his right leg back to the ground. A loud shout from Jin, an aggressive sound that means harm, and he's running right to his only son, death in his eyes.

Get up, Nicky. Get up!

The guys start fighting the triad members. Punches are thrown, and I don't even wince when I see Logan snap a goon's arm without breaking a sweat. I'm shoved back behind Dom, taking a protective stance so no one can get to me, and his tall frame is trying to block my sight from Nicky.

"Don't look, mama," he warns for my ears only. His tone is hard and full of pain.

He wants to protect me, but it's Nicky. I can't not look. He's my everything; I'd do the same for each of my men. Dom is suddenly occupied, hissing under his breath as a triad goon swipes a knife at him. He tries to push me up against the wall behind me next to the doorway, but my eyes burn with a vengeance as I see blood bloom from a rip on Dom's t-shirt. I grip the gun tucked into Dom's belt from behind, ready to start a bloodbath by open firing, but Tey saves the day before I can even pull the trigger. I shake my head, tucking the gun in my boots, and wince. I feel it slide down my knee to my ankle.

I'm probably going to end up shooting myself in the leg, but the knee-high boots are tight enough that the gun settles. I get distracted for a hot second as Tey repeatedly stabs the guard who attacked Dom, his face almost savage and lethal as he drives the knife deep with blood coating his hand. With the guys busy and fighting for our fucking lives, I slip out behind Dom to the side, unaware, and watch Nicky still in the center of the circle, now on his feet again.

I breathe a sigh of relief, collapsing my shaking body against the doorframe. Nicky looks fucking pissed off, and the anger fuels him as he blocks two punches from Jin with his forearms. He retaliates with a swift kick to Jin's upper chest near his armpit, no doubt breaking a rib. Jin stumbles, choking on his breath, and tries to avoid the knee, aiming toward his kidneys, but he's too slow. Nicky raises his knee four times, hitting the same spot as he wraps his arms around Jin's back to hold him in place.

"End this, Nicky!" I shout, hardly noticing as the triad stops fighting and warily watches the fight between father and son.

It's obvious now that Jin isn't as powerful as he thinks he is.

"This is for my mother," Nicky shouts, bringing his arms up and fisting them together before quickly bringing them back down hard on Jin's back.

The sound of Jin's face planting the mats echoes, and his triad backs up slowly until every last one of them stands in front of the walls in silence with bowed heads.

How the tables have turned. Jin just lost his triad in a matter of minutes, which shows no one respects him as a leader.

Dom quickly turns his head to look at me behind him, his shoulders sagging in relief as he sees I'm okay, still in one piece. He wipes blood off the corner of his mouth from an uppercut fist he received before fully straightening to his height and turning back around to watch the end of the fight.

Tey is across the room, silently walking to Nicola, but he watches Nicky like a hawk. He really does love fiercely, and I think Tey would sacrifice himself to save the ones he loves. Dalton follows after him, glaring at the men who held Nicola captive. They actually wince and bow their heads deeper in shame.

"It looks like Nicky has an army at his disposal," Logan comments, crossing his arms and stepping near Nicky in a sign of support for whatever decision he makes.

"This is for Nicola," Nicky growls, kicking his foot out and rolling Jin on his back, so he has no choice but to stare up at his son in defeat.

Nicky grabs the collar of Jin's shirt and punches him in the face until blood spurts from his broken nose. He doesn't stop even as Jin groans in pain, his eyes already developing dark bruises.

"You are down at my feet, old man. Admit defeat. Say it," Nicky says calmly. But it's an act; his chest is heaving as he struggles to maintain his composure.

I just want to wrap my arms around him and never let go. I just might.

"You win," Jin chokes out, spitting up blood and glaring with so much hate that I shiver as I lean heavier against the doorframe.

Nicky drops him back to the mat with a rough shove and turns away to address the triad as they all, one by one, take a knee while keeping their heads bowed.

"Pledge yourself right now. Or join Jin in the shipping container across the seas," Nicky threatens, watching with sharp eyes as each triad member makes loud sounds of agreement, like the beat of a drum that echoes off the walls until I feel it vibrating in my chest.

I grin as Nicola runs at Nicky and throws herself in his arms with a sob. Except everyone isn't watching Jin now since he's propped up on his knees with his head also bowed, like the rest of the triad. I'm watching, though, and my brows are pinched in confusion as I see Jin's shoulder shaking.

Is he crying?

No!

"Fucking die," Jin cackles like a madman, desperate.

His head slowly comes up at the same time as his hand, pointing his gun at Nicky and Nicola with a manic snicker. My eyes focus hard on the finger on the trigger, feeling like everything is moving in slow motion, but I know it's happening in seconds. A loud bang fills my eardrums, making me cover my ears with a scream, but I can't look away.

It's just like in the movies when the body goes flying back from impact, and their actual smoke clouds my vision. I stand in shock as Jin's upper body flies backwards with a bullet hole right between his eyes, and blood immediately pools around his body as Nicky clings his sister to his body in a death grip.

I see something moving out of my peripheral vision, and I slowly turn my head in shock to see Franco leaning against the opposite side of the doorframe while grasping his stomach.

Blood soaks through his fingers, and he drops the gun as he staggers forward toward a shocked Logan.

Franco pauses at my side and glances at me out of the corner of his eye, grimacing in pain like every moment is agony. It probably is, though I can't seem to feel bad.

"I'm sorry. For everything," he says to me in a sincere voice, and I realize Franco isn't one to atone for his sins, so I can only nod and look at Logan.

"Franco? Why?" Logan rasps, his eyes hardening at the exchange, and watches with a raised brow as his father limps weakly over to him.

"I'm sorry, son. I know it's too lat-late, but it's all I can give," Franco chokes out, his legs shaking, before he collapses on his knees next to Logan and Dom.

Nicky and Nicola have their foreheads together as they whisper in hushed tones, watching as Tey toes Jin's body to make sure he's dead. Dalton rolls his eyes and gazes around until he connects his stare with the two guards who took Nicola hostage. He crooks his index and middle fingers at them and says something while pointing at Jin. They wince with quick bows at the waist and nod before bending down to grab each side of Jin's dead body under his limp arms. Jin's blood leaves a trail as they take his body away and out a different door across the room.

"I can't or won't forgive you, but I'll make sure you look like a hero. The people don't need to know that you were corrupted; they need hope. This is a mercy kill, father." Logan sighs in defeat, shaking his head, and I know he wishes things were different.

I watch with tears in my eyes, feeling sad for my heartbroken Lo. I'm fixing it any way I can, no matter what. He won't know heartache while with me. I hold that pumping vessel in the palm of my hands and plan to always guard it.

Logan looks away as a tear trails down Franco's cheek before he nods once in acceptance. Dom clasps Logan's shoulder, and they share a silent conversation as honey eyes meet deep brown. An agreement, one that shows you aren't alone. Enemies to friends. Logan doesn't say anything as he walks away, going to stand next to Nicky and Nicola with his back turned away from Franco.

Tey and Dalton clasp his shoulders in support, leaning their foreheads against his so he doesn't have to suffer alone.

I silently cry, loving and hating this moment. Brothers for life, always have one another's back. You aren't alone. Lean on me.

Dom gazes down at Franco with a look that almost resembles pity for a man who was once strong but ended up pathetic with the path he ran toward at full speed without thinking of the consequences.

"Goodbye, Franco," Dom whispers and withdraws his gun from his holster, leveling the barrel at Franco's head as he gazes up at him with a plea to end his suffering.

"Helena. I'm coming home," Franco whispers one last time, and I have to look away. Only I don't hear the bang of the gun.

A white fabric comes into my vision. It covers both my mouth and nose, the smell of chlorine filling my nostrils as a voice speaks softly in my ear.

"You're mine, little bird."

My limbs instantly go heavy, my heart slowing down as I'm dragged through the doorway behind me unnoticed, and my world is tipped upside down just before everything starts to grow fuzzy and blurry.

Help.

I can see the back of Cruz's dirty jeans and his just as dirty, muddy biker boots as he quietly takes the stairs without anyone stopping him.

I open and close my mouth, wondering why I can't

scream and shout to the rooftops that I'm being taken by a sociopath.

Everyone was busy, so much happening at once that no one noticed I was being taken away.

What the hell did he give me? My limbs feel so heavy, and my throat is like cotton as everything around me feels like it's moving too fast. The next thing I know, I hear a pop and I'm being lowered into a dark hole. The fabric of the carpet under me is sensitive to my skin and causes a slight hiss to escape between my teeth. I want to recoil as Cruz sweeps my hair away from my hair and pets my cheek. Vomit climbs up my throat as I become dizzy at the feel of his hands on me.

"There, there, Tillie. I'm here and will never leave your side again. No one can take you away from me," Cruz says in a voice that's sickeningly obsessed and not in love like he thinks he is. "Take a nap. We'll be leaving all of this behind soon enough," he says as he steps back with a crooked yet not quite a genuine smile as he reaches over head.

He put me in a fucking trunk. Why am I always being kidnapped and shoved in a trunk?

I whimper as I'm entirely plunged into darkness as the trunk lid snaps shut and I can't do anything at the moment since my body isn't cooperating with me.

Tears run down my face as the engine roars to life, the vibrations shaking me and echoing in my ringing ears as I silently cry.

Please help me. Somebody. Anyone but Cruz.

Dom

My hand ricochets back from the gun going off, making me clutch the heavy metal tightly as the bullet penetrates through Franco's skull. I don't regret listening to Franco's last breath; he killed my father. He was just a puppet for bigger schemes, a foot soldier to Jin.

This was for my father and Logan, the brother I always wanted. I will respect his wishes if he wants to make Franco look like a good guy, even when I disagree. I'd rather see him as the villain, a corrupt cop who deserved what he got. Anyone who has ever hurt a loved one would end up in the same position as Franco.

God. I'm so fucking tired. I need to sleep for a couple hours, or years.

"Clean this up and dispose of the bodies. You know what to do," Nicky demands, his eyes as cold as steel as he addresses his triad.

His men still haven't removed their eyes from the ground, waiting on command with nervous gulps. I'd be nervous and curious about what my fate holds for me. None of these men have ever stood up for Nicky or lent a helping hand. But I get it. It's a fucking obey-or-be-killed kind of world sometimes. I'm a hard ass on my men because I have to be if I want them to respect me and follow orders.

"Where did my buttercup get off to?" Tey asks, searching the room with furrowed brows as he fidgets in place.

"What?" I almost shout, clearing my throat to calm down, even though my palms start to sweat when I can't find her as I spin in a circle, looking in every direction.

The triad bows deeply and straightens up to bow over Nicky's outstretched hand to place a kiss on the gold ring on his index finger.

"Has anyone seen her?" Dalton growls out, the noise more beast than man.

Each triad member shakes their heads and silently gets to work, mostly trying to stay invisible as they pick up Franco's body.

More men get up to leave, and some return with a mop and buckets to sweep up the dark liquid of blood on the mats.

"She wouldn't leave us here, not after that. Dom, you're with me. Search the building. Tey, stay here with them." Logan lifts his chin at Nicky and Nicola, but that's not the only reason.

Logan turns his head slightly to look at me with a tilt of his chin toward the stairway with an undisturbed expression, yet I can see the hints of pain, sorrow, anger, and worry all in a rapid flash of his light eyes.

"We'll be back. Dalton, call in some reinforcements and get them to take Nicola to see her boyfriend," I order quickly over my shoulder, following Logan through the open doorway.

"Is he..." Nicola whimpers, her question going unspoken, but Nicky understands.

"He'll be okay. He's just really banged up, but the morphine should help big time," Nicky reassures Nicola, his voice going quiet as his sister sobs in his arms.

"Don't fear, little tiger. Evan is with Doc, and he'll make sure your boyfriend's face stays pretty. He's in good hands," Dalton promises, and I can almost hear him wink from the top of the stairwell.

The moment the door bangs shut behind us, Logan and I are jogging down the three floors without trying to kill ourselves by tripping.

"She has to be around here somewhere." I can't tell if Logan is talking to me or trying to convince himself.

I already know what we will find on the ground, or lack thereof. Tillie would never abandon us, especially when we needed her the most. My gut twists, my pulse going frantic with fear that she's gone.

"What the fuck!" Logan exclaims, drawing in a sharp breath at what lies in a heap at the glass front doors.

"Who is that- Jesus Christ—it's Rig!" Logan drops to his knees with a loud crack of his bones and frantic, worried hands flailing everywhere.

"Take a deep breath. She knows you'd move heaven and hell for her, and that includes making decisions for her old man." I inhale deeply and exhale until his breathing gets under control from my copied movements.

"This is going to break her. Is he…?" Logan asks, running a hand through his thick hair with shaky hands.

"He'll live," I add with conviction in my voice, even though I don't fucking know because Rig looks dead except for the faint flutter of his pulse on his neck.

Thank God for fucking small ass miracles. If Tillie lost Rig, she'd lose a piece of herself, even though she's the strongest woman I know. It would break her, a small chunk of the armor she wears daily.

"Cruz has her," Logan says in a dead voice. The lack of emotion lets me know he is considering the worst-case scenario, but I can't blame him.

I'm doing the same thing.

I grab my cell and hit the speed dial until my street runner answers on the second ring.

"Dom. What's up, Esa?" Gabriel asks all business, which is why I trust him to run the supplies when I'm out of the *Office.*

"I need eyes and ears on the ground. He took my woman. Get everyone on board. I don't fucking care if they are high or not, just get it done," I command into the phone, feeling my pulse pound in my eardrum.

"Who has your queen, boss?" he asks a second later, likely in shock that someone would think of taking my queen away from me.

"Dirty, greasy blond. Cold, dead blue eyes and the Prez of the Joker Demons. Kill the fucker on sight, but make sure Tillie is on-site first before shots are fired. She's my number one priority. Spread the word 'shoot to kill'. His name is Cruz." I lean over Rig as I put the phone on speaker and lift his eyelid to see how respon-sive he is.

Wide brown eyes, so much like my mama's eyes, look back at me, dilated but coherent.

"Whe- where am I?" Rig asks in panic, his voice croaking and dry lips probably from dehydration.

Damn. He looks like he's seconds away from the grave. He's malnourished, bruised, and weak as a newborn cow, with deep bruising and sunken eyes.

"You'll be okay, Rig. Try to stay calm." Logan finally

speaks, shaking his head and inhaling loudly to stay in control.

"Get someone over to Jin's dojo quickly. Rig needs medical attention, an IV bag, pain medications, and a fucking therapist after being in Cruz's hands for so long. A blood transfusion is also required, since he is bleeding profusely from a severed finger," I bark out order after order, because I'm not letting this man die on me.

Tillie needs him.

"How-how do you kno-know me?" Rig asks warily, tired, as he shifts his nervous gaze back and forth between Logan and me.

"We, uh, know Tillie," Logan coughs out, looking away and making it awkward as hell.

"My daughter. He has her. Please. Don't let him hurt her anymore. Please. I'll do anything, but don't let my daughter suffer anymore." Rig sobs and coughs on a wet inhale with lungs that don't sound so good.

"We'll take care of Cruz. Can you tell us anything about where you've been?" I ask as patiently as possible, while glancing at my wristwatch.

It's been ten minutes. She can be anywhere.

God, please.

I'm only asking for this one-time prayer. Please don't take her away from me. I love her. I need her like I need oxygen—that deep part inside me that only allows me to breathe when she's near.

"S-so colddd. Sal-salt. A loud eng-engine," Rig trembles out weakly, lifting his hand to grasp my arm as he tries to lift his upper body off the ground.

"Calm, amigo. Breathe slowly, in and out," I whisper, placing my hand over his thin, papery forearm and looking him in the eye until he starts to breathe easier.

"Nicky might be able to track her down." I lift a brow at Logan, confused, but don't ask because I don't give a shit as long as he has a way of finding her.

"Less than five minutes out, boss," Gabriel mumbles quietly through the phone, having listened to the whole exchange.

"Drive faster. We are heading out in less than a minute tops," I reply and hang up without waiting for an answer; he will make it happen because I said so.

"She's not here. Cruz. Get downstairs now and pull up the app to track her." Logan speaks harshly into the phone with glazed eyes, staring intently out the window before going pale.

"Fuck!" he shouts suddenly, picking up the nearest object, which happens to be a metal chair, and throwing it at the window behind me.

The tinkling of glass at my back doesn't surprise me. Witnessing Logan's rage is like looking at a calm and cool gorilla in its environment until something or someone disturbs the creature. Anyone in its path will most likely die as it destroys and kills until it feels safe again.

"Feel better?" I ask dryly, ignoring him as he scuffs beside me as I look over Rig's injuries.

He'll live. That's all that matters.

"Stay alive for her, old man. You'll see her soon, and she's going to fuss over you, so get better. She doesn't need to worry anymore," I address Rig as he nods his head weakly and slumps on the floor with a quiet groan of defeat.

"Tell her I love her, will you?" he croaks out and stares up at me pleadingly, his eyes so much like Tillie's breaking my heart.

"Tell her yourself," I say, hardening my voice so he

knows that he can't give up when he's so close to having his daughter back in his life.

"I like you. Treat my girl well, and I won't ever have to kill you," he rasps out and closes his eyes on a deep breath, although the corner of his mouth lifts into a tiny smile as Logan opens his big mouth.

"Don't ever leave her again, and I won't have to kill *you*," Logan growls in annoyance, pacing back and forth, most definitely jealous that Rig didn't say he liked him.

I can't stop my eye roll and chuckle as I climb to my feet as the sound of loud, stomping feet comes from the stairwell with raised voices.

"I don't think I like him. But keep him safe. It'd hurt my girl's heart if something happened to the man she loves," Rig says in a serious tone, his dry sense of humor amusing me for the time being.

"Men," Logan whispers with a snort and strides through the broken window, glass crunching under his expensive Italian leather shoes.

"Jesus." Rig chokes out a wet cough and sighs like a father out of his depth with a daughter.

"Don't worry. We all love her, and she loves us," I promise and glance over to see Dalton and Tey on either side of Nicky as they hold him up under his armpits.

"How many men does my daughter have exactly falling at her feet?" Rig gasps out, his eyes opening wide in shock at the sudden appearance of Nicola leaning over his prone body on the ground.

"Five. But only the best for my- cocks! -bestie," Nicola simply supplies, ignoring as Rig coughs in shock. "There there. You must be Daddy?" she asks with a tilt of her head and must be seeing Tillie's eyes staring back at her.

"I'm her Daddy, and well, *Papi* over here too," Dalton grumbles out, his voice just like the rumble of an engine.

"Okay, yeah. We'll just be going now." Tey shifts awkwardly on his feet, making me raise my eyebrow in shock as he seems unable to meet Rig's stare.

"Her location is pinging. Let's move out. Nicola, stay here and get one of Dom's men to give you a ride to see Evan, but, I repeat, don't leave his side until I see you again," Nicky orders, his gaze zig-zags over the phone screen, the bright light reflecting in his eyes until he looks up at his sister for confirmation.

"Yeah, yeah. I'm not going anywhere. I'll just stay here with Daddy Rig and keep him company until then. We'll be fine. The triad won't do anything; they're too scared of your ass now." Nicola waves her hand absentmindedly and shifts closer to Rig to stare instantly into his confused eyes.

"Let's head out. Time to get our girl." I nod toward the parking lot, seeing Gabriel's Mustang and more of my crew members pulling up.

"You got anything strong to drink around here, girl? I think this is more trauma to add to my list, and I need a stiff drink," Rig says as we walk through the missing front window. I barely hear her reply but can't help laughing at what she says.

"I have some." I glance over my shoulder to see her arms gesturing around wildly and snapping her fingers at Tey as he walks by with Nicky. "Gimme that shot of whiskey you have in your boot, TeyTey."

Tey almost trips over his feet and sputters with a nervous chuckle while quickly reaching into his boot to literally pull out a few shot bottles of some expensive whiskey to lay near Rig's head before he practically carries Nicky outside.

"I never thought I'd see the day when Tey is nervous of anyone," Dalton says out loud, which is what we are all probably thinking.

I don't know Tey that well, but I do know he's very comfortable in his skin and doesn't give a shit what anyone thinks of him.

"Shut the fuck up," Tey grunts, tightening his arm around Nicky's waist so most of the pressure is off his ribs the more he leans on his boyfriend's side. "That's the real MVP back there, the original daddy, who means a lot to our girl. We can't fuck that up, so stop with the daddy shit with him. I can already see future dinners. One where Tillie asks her daddy to pass the salt, and you two try passing it around the table to her instead of her real father." Tey glares at Dalton and me until we both agree in nods to his satisfaction.

Life's a real bitch sometimes, and she likes to play cruel, cruel jokes. I'm still going to be her *papi* but I guess I'll have to cool it around the old man.

I shake myself out of my thoughts and meet Gabriel near my car as more of my crew jog into the building to help Rig.

"Boss. We'll take it from here. Go get your queen. Make that fucker suffer." Gabriel clasps me on the back two times with respect and continues walking away without a reply.

Good man.

"Where are we heading?" Logan demands hotly after slamming the passenger door of my Mustang and taps his fingers on his knee with impatient movements.

"Eastbound, on the highway, and going fast. Shit. He just got off the ramp. Heading straight for the ocean, it looks like. He's driving the coastal view streets." Nicky mumbles out directions rapidly as I peel out of the parking lot and gun it down the crowded streets.

"Which marina is close by?" Logan asks, his tone distracted and deep in thought.

"East Pointe, Sea Life Marina, and Golden Yacht Marina..." Nicky trails off, swearing under his breath in Japanese; he sounds fucking pissed.

"What?" Dalton demands on Nicky's other side, his gaze meeting mine in the rearview mirror in confusion.

"Son of a bitch! This whole time, that fucker has been hiding out at the marina." Logan swears in Italian, my car echoing with both of their languages and making me feel like I'm missing something significant.

"Calm down, Nicholas. Deep breath, baby," Tey mutters quietly behind my seat, comforting Nicky until his rough exhales are normal again.

"I'm calling in backup. I don't like not knowing what we are getting into," Dalton grumbles darkly, and I can see his phone screen light brightening the backseats as he types a quick message. "Where am I sending the club?" he asks with an exhausted sigh, probably feeling like this will never end.

When will our girl finally be safe?

"Golden Yacht Marina is where Cruz has been staying. It's the only thing that makes sense," Logan says, staring straight ahead out the window shield, his knee starting to bounce with nerves, which makes my palms sweat.

I don't like this gut feeling.

"How do you know?" I ask through gritted teeth, pressing my foot down on the petal, zooming by honking cars, but not giving a damn if I side-swipe another vehicle as long as we make it in time to Tillie.

"Jin has, I mean, had a yacht in that marina. And Cruz is currently turning into the entrance." Nicky groans, gasping for breath, and hunches over into Tey's side.

"Fuck!" Dalton mutters quietly, his fingers flying over his phone screen.

"We'll get there. She's okay. She's ours, and we protect what's ours," Tey whispers over and over behind me, maybe trying to comfort all of us or himself.

I only know if we take too long to get to her, that yacht can sail anywhere over the seas and we'll never see our girl again.

"Drive faster, Dom." Logan's tone comes out dark, on edge, and almost to the point of frantic.

"I am. I'll get us there in time," I promise with conviction in my tone, and I start praying for the first time in a long time.

Please, God, keep her safe until we can get to her.

I repeat that prayer over and over the whole way to the marina, hardly remembering the drive there. I drove from point A to point B on autopilot, as my stomach tightened with the kind of fear that consumes you whole. The kind you can't stop thinking about, wondering about, and analyzing every possible outcome.

I turn on the street of Golden Yacht Marina, going a little too fast as I jerk the steering wheel and come to a stop with a smoking tailpipe and screeching tires. Car doors open and slam, all of us waiting on Nicky's lead as he stares at his phone, cursing in Japanese again.

"What?" I bark, feeling my heart pound so hard as if it wants to jump out of my chest cavity and flop around until it just stops.

"They are already out on the water, moving fast and heading southeast." Nicky slumps against Tey, his face panicking as he looks at all of us.

"Fuck this. Who knows how to drive a boat?" Logan asks, pacing back and forth with his hands on his hips in anger.

"Oh hell. We might die, but I have a club brother who can," Dalton groans and swipes a hand down his face as we hear a rumble of engines getting closer and closer until motorcycles are loudly ringing in my ears.

"It doesn't matter how well he can steer a fucking boat. We need to go now before she's too far ahead. Once she crosses a certain part of water, trading begins, and literal pirates take over the sea of those parts," Nicky explains, sweat covering his brow as he gasps and holds his ribs.

"Okay, okay. Axel is driving. Nicky, you should stay here-," Logan starts, but Nicky cuts him off with an icy glare.

"I'd like to see you try," Nicky responds, straightening to his full height, even though it has to hurt.

"Drop it, Lo. You'd be going too, even if you had a bullet embedded into your skin," Tey remarks and rubs Nicky's back absentmindedly, as he peers around at the boats surrounding us.

Axel cuts off his bike engine and swings his leg over the seat before quickly striding over to us to stand next to Dalton.

"What do you need, Prez?" his club brother asks, nodding to us before giving Dalton his attention.

"The usual, brother. Stealing a ride, saving our girl, and you're the fucking driver of this fucking little boat," Dalton tells him, clapping him on the back, and starts jogging toward the dock boards.

"We can't take a yacht. We need a small speed boat." Tey keeps looking around and raising a single eyebrow at something off to the right of the docks.

"Lead the way," I say, knowing Tey just found our ride by the mysterious grin on his face that slightly freaks me out.

"It's not going to be pleasant. This type of boat is for stealth and speed." Tey cackles and starts leading the way, with Nicky attached to his side as he limps on his right leg.

"I need a fucking vacation. I'm too young for this shit," Logan mumbles to himself and strides after them while Dalton and Axel walk next to me.

"I'm sure Dalton informed you of the situation with Rig. He made it to Doc?" I ask, trying to distract myself from losing my damn mind as we jog down the docks, passing big yachts until we see rusty fishermen's boats, and then each ship starts to get smaller and smaller than the last.

"Yeah, Doc was just patching up the kid, Evan, just as I was pulling out. Your guys were carrying Rig in at the same time," Axel informs me grimly, probably not liking the state of the boats we walk by and all the shit that went on tonight.

"Good. You think your club doctor can handle it?" I ask Dalton, rolling my eyes as he scuffs at my question like I'm an idiot for even asking.

"Doc knows what he's doing. Both Rig and Evan are in good hands," Dalton replies and groans as he sees where Tey has stopped up ahead. "Fuck my life. We might just die tonight by sinking in the ocean."

"I'm sure your brother here knows how to drive that thing," I point out dryly and take a deep breath before striding past the guys as they argue.

"Get in the fucking boat. We don't have time to waste," I remind them, hearing curses and groans of defeat as I stand at the end of the dock before jumping down into the smallest fucking boat ever as it wobbles under my weight.

I wonder if it will be a quick death as I drown and become shark food?

Guess we'll find out because I'm not stepping back on land until my queen is safely in my arms again.

I'll be lost at sea, searching for her until I die.

That's what a man in love does: go to desperate lengths for his woman.

I swallow thickly as the other guys jump down heavily into the boat, our knees bracing as the boat rocks violently under our weight.

"Might want to hold onto something. This boat is small, but she can go up to a hundred miles per hour. The waves are going to have us flying across the water." Axel gestures to the boat and finds a pair of keys near the helm before starting the engine and, immediately, backing the boat away from the docks.

"Buckle up, buttercups. Going to be a bumpy ride." Tey rubs his hands together with a manic look in his blue eyes as he helps place Nicky into the captain's passenger seat.

"Oh fuck. Oh shit," Dalton mutters and grabs onto one of the bars on either side of the boat just as Axel pulls the clutch forward until we are speeding dangerously in the no-wake zone.

My stomach rolls as the boat jumps speedily over waves, making me sway in place as I grab the metal bar over our heads for balance. I can only see darkness ahead, making it look like the ocean is going to swallow us whole.

I wonder if she's okay. If she's thinking the same thing as me, we could get lost out here, where the night sky blends in with the dark ocean until you can't tell the difference between the two. Lost at sea with no way home.

"We'll get her back," Logan says next to me, looking straight ahead as he holds the back of Nicky's seat and keeps looking over his shoulder at the blinking red dot of Tillie's location.

"Whatever it takes," I whisper, meaning every word as a vow.

CHAPTER 16

Cruz

She looks so beautiful like this. Trails of tears stain her tan cheeks, the shine of wetness making me want to lick her tears up to see if I can taste the emotion. She cries out and reaches out blindly with a swing of her fist. She's so broken and defeated. A bird with clipped wings, unable to fly away ever again from me. I'll keep them disfigured for the rest of her life so she can't run away. I'm all she needs, and all she'll ever want.

"Shh. Shh. Little bird. None of that now. I'll take care of you. Don't you want me to love you?" I ask her, grabbing her wildly swinging wrists and trapping them between her breasts as I lean over the lip of the trunk into her space.

I skim my nose along her jawline, taking a deep breath, and grip her wrists tighter as she struggles harder in my grip.

"Eat shit! You can't love, Cruz. Go to hell." Tillie curls her upper lip as if disgusted by me; I think she really is, and that only causes rage to consume me.

I don't say a word as I lift her roughly out of the trunk, ignoring her pained yelp as her ankle smacks into the hood. Her fists beat weakly against my back the moment she's thrown over my shoulder. Walking down the docks, I keep my pace slow as we pass million-dollar yachts and their sloppy, rich owners who turn their backs on me the moment I make eye contact. No one cares that I have my little bird thrown over my back, her weak pleading whimpers and cries of help ignored. The wealthy mind their own business, not giving a shit if someone is being kidnapped right in front of them, just so long as their expensive, precious money is left alone. I whistle in a jolly tune, hardly feeling any pain as Tillie bites my bicep in a pathetic attempt to hurt me, which only causes me to laugh loudly.

My voice echoes back to me, being heard over the minor slaps of waves against the boats. My laugh has always sounded hollow and empty, missing something, and I think one day I'll find it with my little bird. She's the key to making me feel emotions—maybe to understand sadness and happiness. The only time I've ever felt something related to joy was fucking Tillie in the ass and hearing her cries of pain. Even now, my lip is twitching as I remember carving my knife into her shoulder blade.

"I'll kill you. I promise," Little Bird whispers into my back, a vengeance evident in her tone that makes me believe her.

"You can try, though that will never happen. I'll break every bone in your little body and still use your cunt, even if you're on the brink of death. You are *mine*," I threaten, grinding my teeth as she whispers no repeatedly under her breath while she kicks her feet into my thighs.

Finally, I see my yacht at the end of the dock and walk faster because I want my dick inside her tight cunt to teach her a lesson she'll never forget. It's been a week since I've used my knife, and I plan on carving my name all over her body. My boots make the boards under my feet creak and groan as I jog up the ramp and finally onto the boat. I've been staying here for months, living like the filthy rich with Jin's money. I couldn't give a shit where I stayed, but it brought some sort of good feeling, knowing I was making Jin cater to my needs. I was eating his food, sleeping on his bed, and staining his carpets red as I sliced up his staff. He had to keep sending replacements, probably not knowing or caring why, but still. It gives, well, it *gave* me a thrill when he was alive.

Poor fucking bastard.

I smirk to myself as I let Tillie fall the moment I release my hold on her. She lands ungracefully on the plush, white carpet at my feet. I stand her over like her god, master, and savior as she looks up at me with wide, brown, scared eyes.

"Shh, shh, Little Bird. All will be okay once we are far away from here, so no one can take you away from me again. You won't run, will you?" I question her, startling a yelp from her as I grasp her long hair and shake her head roughly.

I can't help it. I get so fucking mad when I think of her running away again. Making me chase after her. It's as if she wants me to hurt her.

"Tell me you won't leave and that you love me." I grind my teeth, shaking her head once more as she cries out in pain and scrambles to wrap her fingers around my wrist to ease the pressure.

"No." She stubbornly lifts her chin, glaring up at me as if she has a choice.

Oh well. I'll have her kissing my feet very soon enough and telling me she loves me after every other word that comes out of her fuckable mouth.

"No? We'll see about that. It's a real shame that I'll have to keep you on a tight leash for a while until you learn your lesson. You'll be seeing my face everywhere, Little Bird. From the moment you wake up, when you have to take a piss. And when I feel like feeding you, you'll take the food I give you from my hands with this disobedient mouth." I grip her chin harshly, squeezing as tears fill her eyes and caress her bottom lip. "You and I are going to be tied together for a long time. You'll get used to my face between your legs and my cock fucking your pussy every day whenever I feel like it."

I release her with a shove, the vein throbbing on my forehead as she shakes her head continuously and wraps her arms around her stomach.

She'll learn quickly. I'm not a patient man, and if I don't have use for something any more, I dispose of it.

"Fuck. Stop crying, you cunt. Get up." I growl in annoyance, grabbing her wrists impatiently and dragging her to her feet when she fights me every few inches.

"No. Fucking stop! I won't let you—never again," she cries out, trying to yank her arm out of my hand as I walk out of the gallery of rich mahogany and gold accents decorated on every surface.

Fucking rich people.

"Get used to living like the rich for a few days while you can. Once we get to Russia, I will teach you why you should never run away from me again," I tell her, my voice sounds unhinged and obsessive to my own ears.

"Rus-Russia?" she stutters, fear evident in her tone, which gives me a rush of endorphins.

"No one will help you, especially where we are headed. Step out of line, and I'll freely let men destroy your pussy before you come crawling back to me." My facial expression remains blank as I stare down into her huge pupils that keep shrinking and expanding in terror.

"What about the rest of the Demon Jokers?" she asks with a shiver, climbing on unsteady legs behind me as I continue walking out onto the side deck of the yacht and leading us to the stairs to the captain's cabin.

"They are a joke. I've never cared one way or another about the club; it was never my end goal. Being president to a bunch of Neanderthal fools wasn't part of my plans. Since the moment I met you, I knew I had to have you," I confess, furrowing my brows as an unhinged giggle escapes her.

I only ever speak the truth, so why would she think that's funny? Did she think I shared her with the club brothers to be cruel? No, I did that to teach her a lesson that, in the end... I'll be the one who has her last. It never matters who her first is; I'll be right there to set her straight every time she's bleeding on the floor.

"You're sick. Fucking delusional," she hisses between her teeth, her arm practically vibrating in my hand as I tighten my grip until I know it will leave bruises.

"I might be sick, but that's because of you. It's your fault I'm this way. I love you!" I swirl around once we reach the top deck and grab her shoulder to shake her as I yell in her face.

"You plan on throwing her overboard before you get to fuck her?" Nix asks behind me in amusement, his cigar clouding the air around us.

I realized I had backed her into the railing, shaking her roughly enough that her head snapped back as her upper body was draped halfway over the ledge.

"Fuck! Look what you do to me!" I release her, running my hands through my hair as I pace back and forth in front of her, and she collapses with a gasp to her knees.

"Fuck you," she rasps out, her chest heaving while narrowing her eyes with rage, taking over her features.

My fists clench at my sides, distantly hearing Nix chuckle behind me as she talks back to me. I turn around and look at him, half emerging from the shadows near the captain's pit. His bearded face split in a grin, the cut running over his right eye making him look menacing as he stares at Tillie while licking his lips.

The sick fuck. He doesn't love her or want to live mentally in her mind like me, but he does want her body. He taught her how to ride a bicycle, watched her grow up, and fucked her at the first chance he got.

"You know what? Let this lesson be one to remember, Little Bird." I curl my lip in a sneer as I look down at her, still on her knees at my feet, almost pathetic except for the fire burning in her gaze.

"Need some help, Prez?" Nix asks, his tone laced with dark intent and desire.

I keep my gaze on Tillie as I answer him, feeling my cock harden as she pales to the point of looking like she's going to vomit.

"You know what? I think I do need some help with Little Bird. She's already on her knees, so you might as well use this to your advantage."

"Oh, you got it, Prez. She has a wide mouth. I want to stuff it full," Nix says with a chuckle and walks over to stand right in front of her kneeling position, causing me to step back and watch her suffer at another man's hands.

It's different seeing her pain than pleasure. At least I know she's getting so traumatized from this that she'll practically be begging for me to take her instead of any other man.

I can handle my rage, obsession, and wanting her heart for myself as long as she doesn't enjoy herself. I'll lose my mind if that happens. Her moaning for another man and begging like a whore would send me over the edge. I know this, and I think she does too, as she stares around Nix with a hateful glare in my direction.

I'll kill her and keep her heart locked in a chest forever.

She'll never leave me, no matter what.

CHAPTER 17

Tillie

Bile rises up my throat, causing me to choke back a gag as Nix's pants legs fill my vision. He's the last of the club's brothers that raped me before Cruz. To see and smell him standing this close causes me to sway on my knees, willing myself to not pass out. I'd rather be awake than unconscious and not know what's being done to my body. Strong smells of cigars make me choke back another round of vomit in my throat, and a dirty stink of motor grease mixed in uncleanness from not showering for days.

Oh God.

I pant for breath, trying to desperately draw in air as I slightly turn my head to the side to inhale the salty smell of the ocean. It's so dark out here, the boat gliding over the waves on a moonless night for endless miles. I'm completely at their mercy. I whip my head back around when I hear a zipper lowering with a rusty chuckle from Nix. Okay, I can do this and then have time to think once the deed is done. It's not something I haven't been through before. I'm strong, and I can think of the guys as I drift further and further away from land and sanity.

"That's a good little cunt. Open your mouth," Nix says,

fisting a handful of my hair and pulling sharply so my face is pressed against the roughness of his jeans as his semi-hard cock grazes my cheek. I whimper quietly as my eyes water, not wanting to go through this again, but sometimes we don't have a choice in the matter of what we need to do to survive. I know Cruz is watching somewhere behind Nix; it's all a fucking test and expressing his way of *love*. It's bullshit. This isn't love; it's a passion to control someone you're obsessed with to the point of being unhealthy. Well...

Fuck him, and fuck this!

I lean around Nix, hissing in pain as I feel strands of my hair pull from Nix's grip. I hardly feel it, though, as I make eye contact with Cruz and put every ounce of loathing I feel for him in my expression before breaking our gazes to look back up at Nix. I force a sweet smile and nuzzle my cheek into his cock with a pleased hum in my throat, as if I'm really enjoying this.

I fight back the strong urge to gag. This is the only way to send Cruz off the deep end and hopefully end up killing Nix.

"Oh God, your cock is so big, Nix. Do you want me to suck it?" My tone comes out breathless, in awe, and drawing Cruz's attention with each raspy word leaving my mouth.

"Fuck. You cock sucking bitch. Put my dick in your mouth and enjoy it." Nix groans as I give him a broad lick at the base of his penis while keeping eye contact, knowing he can't look away.

I feel sick to my stomach and dizzy. I wonder if this type of hurt deep inside of me will ever end. Maybe I'm meant to burn in hell always, endless torture of the same thing over and over that I won't be able to tell what's real or not. The only thing that keeps me going right now is my guys. I know they won't judge me for what I must do to survive, only so I can see them again.

"That's it. Give it another lick. You really love cock, don't you whore?" Nix groans again in pleasure from above and doesn't hear the wood dock flooring creak right by his side.

I allow the saliva to pool between my lips and slide out as I lick Nix again. I'm hoping the taste of him leaves my mouth before I can taste a hint of him on my tongue. Heavy breathing like an angry bull fills the silence. Besides Nix's loud grunts and groans, my stare shifts to the side, and Cruz's eyes meet the cold, icy blue, staring down at me with a sneer.

"Do you love him, Tillie? Does he get your pussy wet?" Cruz shouts so loudly Nix jumps and stumbles away when he notices the raging, hot fury in Cruz's gaze as it falls on him. "I said you could punish her, not make her enjoy it!"

It happens so fast, but I act without thinking.

Cruz pushes Nix hard on the chest just as I shift my body into a tight ball and duck down with my head smacking against the floor while trying to protect my body by folding my arms protectively over my head. The air rushes out of me as Nix's legs collide with my ribs as he starts to tip backwards over my crouched position. I glance up between my long hair to see his arms windmilling as he tries to catch his balance, but he doesn't stand a chance with me in the way. It only took one rage-fueled push from Cruz, and Nix is flipping backwards over the railing, falling below in the darkness of the ocean. Not before we hear a loud thunk, before a splash sounds. He must have hit something on the way down. He didn't even have time to scream.

I choke on a sob that is crawling up my throat, slowly lowering my arms as I peek between the curtains of my long hair. Cruz stands in front of me, not blinking as he stares down at me and pulls his hair while releasing a scream of frenzy rage.

"You did this! You want to get your pussy wet for another man and beg for it? Fine! Your cunt will never be empty again, fucking whore." He eerily relaxes his expression, all emotions vanishing in a second.

My stomach turns, and I end up throwing up at his feet, uncaring about the smell or mess of bile. He's going to pass me around and let strangers use my body over and over. I dry heave until nothing else comes up. I sob and choke as he grabs my forearm in a bruising grip that causes me to whine at the burn. He walks in a ridged, clipped stride up to the last set of stairs that lead up to the third upper dock. We pass the captain's cockpit, and I notice it empty, wondering who's steering the yacht before I'm being dragged up the slippery and wet stairs.

It's an odd thing to notice; it's the only part of the boat I've seen that is wet, along with the outline of a set of shoe prints. Maybe it was Nix or the Captain. I realize I'm trying to distract myself, pulling my mind away from what's happening at this very moment.

I can feel myself shutting down as I look out into the dark sea, wondering how far away from land we are. There isn't a light in sight from any direction, as if we are the only ones out here. I'm alone with Cruz. I think it sinks in at that point. My head stays turned down to the floor as I shuffle my feet. I feel like my whole body hurts. I really do think this is my body shutting down.

"What the fuck?" Cruz says in shock. I've never heard that tone from him before at all.

I almost bump into Cruz's back and try to stop my whole body from shaking in uncontrollable terror. What waits for me now? I think I'll take my chances with the ocean at this point. I'm starting to think I'll never see my guys again, hear their voices, feel their touch, or hear the beat of their hearts as I lay my head against their strong chests.

One tear slides down my cheek as I stare down at my feet in defeat.

Nothing matters anymore.

"Baby girl, you'll raise your head right now and never have to hide again."

I gasp, my head snapping up at the sound of Logan's deep, honeyed voice.

Before I can step in his direction, Cruz twists my wrist and yanks me around him until my back is plastered to his front as he brings his other hand up with his hand gripped around a knife handle that looks oh so familiar.

The last time I saw that blade, it was making me bleed and cutting into my flesh. I hardly feel the blade rest against my throat, the sharp, smooth edge digging into my skin right under my chin. But I couldn't care less. If this was the moment I was to die, I'd be happy.

They're here. They came for me.

"Hi, mama. Don't cry, my queen." Dom says this in a husky voice full of emotion as he stares at me with deep brown eyes.

"You'll die for touching her." Nicky growls, his posture straight and his voice deadly serious.

"Take a deep breath, Tillie. It will be over soon, promise." Dalton steps forward, his hand reaching for me, but stops midair as Cruz presses the knife harder onto my neck, making me hiss in pain at the sudden burn.

I can't help the gut-wrenching sob that crawls up my throat and leaves my parted lips. I can't see Tey, but I know he's somewhere in the shadows, just waiting to pounce. I can practically feel his searing gaze on my body.

"You're here," I choke out, my whole chest shaking in relief.

"Always," Logan speaks up, his eyes watering as he stares deep into my eyes and doesn't look away even as Cruz starts yelling.

"She's not yours. Mine. All mine! I'll kill you all and make her watch; she'll know for the rest of her life that your deaths are in her hands." Cruz's voice comes out menacing and crazy, almost hysterical.

My heart beats rapidly; fear coursing through my veins, but not for myself. I've accepted death long ago, so I'm not afraid of it. But I do fear seeing the people I love no longer walking this earth next to me. Everyone leaves me behind as they go beyond somewhere that I can't follow, and that scares me.

I won't be letting that happen tonight.

The guys' bodies are ridged, posed to attack, but they won't. Not when a knife is digging into my skin, and it takes just one sweep of the sharp blade to end my life.

I am strong. I'm not the victim anymore. He doesn't own me.

I kept repeating that silently to myself, my gaze hardening in determination. No more.

"You'll never have me, Cruz, and I think it's time you acknowledge that through your thick skull." I grind my teeth through the pain as I shift my upper body forward, the knife digging harder into my skin so that it will probably leave a scar later.

I grunt as I swing my head back fast, the back of my skull smacking into Cruz's nose. He curses loudly, and his grip loosens on my waist so that I can shift my hips to the side to jab my elbow into his gut.

The air escapes through his mouth with a groan of pain. At the distraction, I stomp my left foot over his as hard as I can and then hook my ankle over the back of his while shoving my body backwards to tip us both off balance. His knife slides across my throat, the blade just barely kissing my skin and causing it to lightly seep blood from a thin cut. I spin on my heels, breathing hard, and stop lifting my fists in front of me in a pose to attack him with everything inside of me, but I don't have to worry now.

Tey.

"Well, that was fucking hot. I almost want you to repeat that so I can record it for the spank bank and save it for a rainy day." Tey winks at me from over Cruz's shoulder, his biceps straining as he wraps his arms around Cruz in a bear hug.

"Tey," I breathe out and almost collapse, but Logan is suddenly there, catching me as Dalton strides past us with Dom to help Tey.

I bury my face into Logan's chest as he holds me tight to his body, rocking us back and forth as I breathe in his scent of honey and cloves.

"I got you. He can't hurt you again," Logan whispers in my ear and swipes my hair away from my face as I pull away to look up at him.

Nicky is standing by our side, his gaze roaming over my face with a worried expression until his emerald eyes meet mine.

I'm about to explain everything—the guilty feeling curling in my gut about what I did with Nix—but he stops me before I can even open my mouth.

"Don't. I can see it in your eyes. You did whatever you had to do to survive. I'm proud of you; we all are." Nicky's tone is hushed with a hint of pain as he holds his ribs with his arm across his rib cage and strokes the side of my face lovingly with his one, calloused hand.

"You guys saw, didn't you?" I rasp out, blinking my eyelids rapidly to hold the tears back.

"Yes," Logan says, still petting my head and staring down his chest at me curling into him. "We understand, Tillie. It was something you had no control over, but that ends now. This is your decision. What do you want done with him?" he asks, jerking his chin at the grunts and thuds of flesh meeting flesh behind me.

I slowly turn around in his arms and lean against his chest for support as I watch Tey, Dom, and Dalton kick their boots repeatedly into Cruz's curled-up, battered body on the floor. One of them stuffed his mouth with a rag, probably Dalton, since he's always working on his bike and needs something to wipe off the motor grease on his palms.

Cruz's muffled insults and screams of rage are a relief to not be able to hear. Only his angry eyes burn holes into my skull as I look away with a shudder. My eyes glance around the boat, stopping at the object hanging above our heads near the railing.

"Can you guys tie his wrists together and hang him up on that hook?" I ask, tipping my head back to glance up at Logan as he chuckles in utter, dark delight at my plan.

"Oh, you wicked little monster. I like this plan." Tey hops in place, bouncing like a bunny in delight, and I swear to God, he skips over the control box to lower the hook usually used for letting down smaller rafts into the waters.

While he works the hook lower, Dalton and Dom each grab a groaning Cruz and drag him across the floor by his wrists. I don't feel an ounce of pity or guilt at each bruise and probably broken ribs that cover Cruz's body from my guys beating the shit out of him.

"How did you get here? And know where to find me?" I

suddenly ask, turning my head to Nicky, my brow raised as he fingers the dove on the necklace he gave me weeks ago.

"A tracker. I need to know where you are, twenty-four-seven. Knowing you're safe gives me peace of mind, and I don't regret doing it." He leans forward and kisses my lips in the softest, barely there glide of his mouth against mine before pulling away to help the guys hook the rope around Cruz's wrists until the hook is finally lowered.

I watch as Dalton gives a tight tug, satisfied that the ropes will hold, before nodding at a wickedly smiling Tey to bring Cruz up until his feet are only skimming the dock flooring.

"Axel is driving the boat back; he knocked out the captain and will wake him up to glide the boat back onto the docks. I wouldn't want the fucker to try parking this monster of a yacht." Dalton must have heard my other question because he comes over to pull me out of Logan's arms and into his own with a hard squeeze as he lifts me off my feet to swing me around in a circle. "Don't ever leave me again." He breathes deeply into my neck just before he sets me down again to stare into my eyes.

"Never," I promise with watery eyes, wondering what I ever did to deserve these guys.

"How are we doing this, mama? What do you need?" Dom appears at my other side and snatches me out of Dalton's arms to wrap his strong arms around me, pressing little kisses all over my face that make me laugh at the tickling, wet-loving pecks.

"I love you guys so much," I choke out, swallowing and clearing my throat, because I refuse to cry again tonight.

Maybe tomorrow, when everything catches up with me. But for now, it's time I put years of revenge to use, and I think I know just how I will do it.

I stand on my tippy toes and kiss Dom's sharp cheek-bone before falling back on my heels. I pull out of his arms and walk over to Cruz, passing Tey while lightly running my fingertips over the dimple on his cheek before moving on. I stop in front of the man who caused me years of pain and trauma. Someone who made me afraid of my own shadow, scared to run away, and not knowing if he'd hurt me again or kill me. He's just a man. A man who can't feel anything inside and makes awful decisions in life that hurt others. He is a sociopath that can never change, even if he wishes he could.

"You're going to see what it means to love. I'll give you that, but nothing else. This is what the meaning of love looks like and consent." I stand in front of Cruz, letting go of my fear once and for all as I look into his raging, wide blue gaze.

"Yoth fckin bitc-," he mutters through his gag, his meaning clear even if his voice is muffled.

"I am a fucking bitch. But I'm not your fucking bitch," I taunt, dancing backwards as he jerks and wiggles against the ropes, but he's not going anywhere.

I turn back to my guys and see them all with the same posture. Arms crossed over their muscular chests and murderous glares aimed at the broken man behind me.

"Anything?" I ask one more time, making sure, because this will be a lot.

"Yes," Logan answers for them, glancing left and right as my guys nod in agreement.

"I need this. I need you all. Please heal me," I whisper and turn to the right until I can see my guys and Cruz out of the side of my eyes.

I take a deep breath and slowly lower to my knees on the floor, pausing for a second to gather courage. I turn my head toward each of my men and lower myself further onto the floor until my upper chest is flat on the surface, and my ass is sticking straight in the air as I clasp my hands together to raise above my head.

"Tell us what to do," Dalton grumbles, biting his bottom lip as his gaze shifts over my presenting position, which I know is his favorite.

"I need and want you to fuck me. Any hole you want to. I just want to feel you fill me up with your cum. Please. Take me." My voice is low and raspy, and I feel my heart pounding as the guys step forward, almost as one as they look over my body hungrily with heated gazes.

"Are you sure, pet?" Nicky asks thickly, his eyes hungrily devouring my body.

"Yes," I answer simply. I have never been more sure of anything.

I need this to heal inside and out. This is me saying yes to everything they can offer.

I ignore the muffled shouting on my other side and keep eye contact with each of my guys as they stare for a beat longer before Tey steps forward first.

"Whatever you need, peaches. But I need you to do something for me," Tey says, walking over and bending down behind me until I can feel the back of his strong thighs flat against mine.

I shiver. Even though I've felt their skin against mine, I really missed this.

"What?" I ask, gripping my fingers together as I feel his fingers slide over my thighs and up until he's grasping the waistband of my shorts.

"I want you to look over at him and not look away. Can you do that?" Tey asks softly, his tone understanding and loving.

I think about it. I want Cruz to see what the guys can do to my body and soul, but I don't know if I can make eye contact as they fuck me. But I trust Tey, so I'll do it even if it scares me a little.

"Okay, anything you want," I reply and gasp as he slides my shorts down and off in one smooth move that leaves goosebumps in his wake.

"Dangerous words, but don't worry, Killer, I'll make it feel good for you too," Tey promises in a silky whisper near my ear and strokes his fingers back and forth at the crease where my thighs meet my ass cheeks.

"I don't want it to be about me; I just want each of you to come inside me. Take my body as yours; use me; come for me." I gasp at the heated look taking over their faces at each word leaving my mouth, and I know I'm about to be fucked hard.

"But that's... I want to give you pleasure," Tey mutters behind me, clearly confused at my request.

I shake my head with a small laugh, loving him more for this.

"Tey, it's okay. I'm giving you permission to use my body as you please, but I only want you to come. Fill my pussy until your cum is overflowing. Please," I plead with a whisper and whimper with a gasp as he suddenly pushes inside me without warning.

My body sinks into the sensation of his cock piercing grazing my inner walls and thrusting in tiny snaps of his hips until he's bottomed out. He grabs my hair at the base of my neck and tugs up my head to the left until I'm staring into Cruz's eyes.

At first, my body freezes, but Tey relaxes his grip slightly as I lay my cheek on my forearm. I don't understand at first why Tey wants me to look at someone who's caused me so much pain over the years, but I start to get it after he pulls out slowly and thrusts back in just as unhurriedly. It's an addicting, delicious feeling, and even better as the pupil of Cruz's eyes expands in fury.

"Fuck, angel. Your pussy is gripping me so tight. Tell me again how you want me to fill this pussy with my cum." Tey moans, his fingers letting go of my hair, and reach down to grip my hips in both hands.

"I need your cum, Tey. I'm begging." I bite my lip to silence my moan as he curses behind me and snaps his hips sharply forward, his cock pounding into me at a fast pace.

"You want this?" He growls, breathing heavily as he grips my hips tighter but rubs his thumbs back and forth over my skin.

"I love you, Tey. Every time you make me laugh or do something out of the ordinary, it makes me love you even more." My mouth drops open as he fucks me fast and hard, his cock piercing and grazing that spongey tissue inside that feels fucking amazing.

"I love you too, Tillie. You're my everything," he chokes out and shouts as I slam my ass back, meeting his thrusts and dragging his orgasm to the surface.

Warm, sticky cum fills me to the brim and overflows as he quickly pulls out to watch it leak out of my pussy and drip onto the floor under me.

"I can't have this go to waste," Tey mutters in a sexy tone, making me jump in surprise as he gathers the cum dripping out and shoves it back inside. "Maybe this will get you pregnant, finally." I don't need to look back to know that Tey says this to me but is looking directly at Cruz.

I breathe heavily, staying in place, and watch as Tey approaches my other side to stand next to a swinging, suspended Cruz. I don't look away, deciding I need to do this while staring at my nightmare the whole time to prove I'm not the victim anymore. It's working. The rage and defeat are apparent in Cruz's gaze. It only gets better as Tey pulls out his curved knife and plays with it, taunting Cruz with the sharp blade before he swiftly brings it down and stabs Cruz in the thigh. His scream is wet and muffled, but still music to my ears.

Finally, he feels only an ounce of pain I've felt in his care.

"Baby girl, I'm going to fuck you here," Logan says behind me, grazing his fingers through the cum at the opening of my pussy, but he drags his fingers to my puckered hole and rubs cum onto my asshole. "But I'm preparing you here for Dalton."

My insides shake as I lay panting in need, knowing I'll never get tired of this feeling coursing through my veins. Pleasure, pain, and love.

"Please. Fuck me and get me ready for Dalton's big cock, Lo," I beg, moaning loudly as he swiftly fills me, gliding in effortlessly from the mess of cum and how wet I am between my thighs.

Logan fucks like he does with everything in life. Passionate, hard, and intuitive to his surroundings, he is everything my body ever needs.

"That's my good girl. Always so wet for us. Such a good fucking girl," Logan praises, making me cry out as he angles his hips to the right and thrusts upwards.

I can hear the wet, slurping noises of my pussy as he drags his cock out to the tip and pounds back in a punishing, quick fuck.

I love every second.

"I love you, Logan. Your protective and possessive arms will always keep me safe," I say through each thrust with a low grunt as I shift my hip back, feeling every glide of his fat cock.

"I love you too, Tillie. Knew the moment you stepped into my life, I'd be a goner and was never going to turn back." Logan growls out his release, painting my pussy with load after load of white sticky cum.

My lungs expand on an inhale as he slides out, more cum dripping down my thighs and coating my skin in a shiny sheen. I watch through heavy lids as Logan calmly steps away and walks over to Tey, grabbing his knife out of his hand when he holds his palm out. Without saying a word, Logan stares Cruz down with hatred and reaches up to his bound wrists. I don't cringe but just calmly watch as Logan cuts off Cruz's index finger. Blood oozes out quickly, flowing like a river over his wrists. A tear leaks down Cruz's cheek—the first time I've ever seen him express pain or tears.

I draw in a shocked inhale as I'm suddenly flipped onto my back, and Dom's deep brown eyes are staring down at me as he strokes his thumb over my bottom lip.

"Look at him, Tillie. Look at his suffering. He knows you'll never be his," Dom whispers in my ear and thrusts inside me, his nostrils flaring as he feels the gush of cum sliding out of me. Then he draws back, only to push back in just as slowly.

His hips roll against him, my clit rubbing along his pelvic bone with each slide in and out of my pussy. It's slow lovemaking. He wants me to feel every single thrust, the drag of his cock that pushes deeper and deeper until I feel completely full of him. He reaches up and gently turns my head so I'm watching Cruz again. Putting a little bit of pressure on my face, he holds me still as he picks up the slams of his hips against mine. Sweat drips down between my breasts. I arch my back and hear him curse as he hits different spots inside of me. He starts rutting into me. I reach down to his ass and clench him closer.

"Faster. Make me yours. Come for me," I whisper to Dom, my eyes blurry in pleasure, that I don't even see Cruz at this point. "I love you, Dom. Your power and passion leave me in awe. I want you to stalk me forever."

"Oh fuck, mama. I love you, too. I never want to leave this pussy." His accent gets thicker and deeper as he fucks me faster and faster, until his whole body tightens as he starts coming.

He coats my inside so deeply that I can feel each splash that leaves me moaning as he pants above me and slips out of my pussy on the next breath. I'm not empty for even a second before Nicky picks me up with a pained grunt and sets me on his lap on the decking floor. I follow Dom with my gaze as he walks over to Cruz and takes the knife from Logan.

I'm starting to see a pattern. Each cut or stab for each time he's hurt me.

I'm so much in fucking love, my eyes burn with surpressed tears as I turn to Nicky and offer a watery smile at him as he pushes my hair over my shoulder. He doesn't say anything as he grabs my hips and positions me over his hard cock. Lowering my body on his cock, I moan in plea-sure, feeling the pressure behind my belly button as I sink all the way down on him.

"Ride me, pet. Make me come," Nicky orders with a smirk on his lips as he sees my chest turn pink at the command.

He knows I love following his orders, only rewards await me every time.

"Will you leave me sore and fill me up so I can feel you

for days? Please?" I ask, adding please when he lifts a dark eyebrow, and he only answers by moving his hands around my waist and to my ass cheeks.

He grabs my ass in each hand, squeezing and adding a light slap that makes me sharply roll my hips at the feeling of pain and pleasure mixing.

"Since you asked so nicely. Ride me hard and fast, pet. Let me see these tits bounce for me," Nicky says, reaching up and sliding his thumbs over both of my nipples, which harden and tingle.

I roll my hips in a figure eight and lean my body further into him until my head is leaning against his shoulder with my arms wrapping around his upper back. My gaze is once again on Cruz. I know he sees every thrust of my hips moving back and forth on Nicky's cock as he wraps his arms around my waist to hug me to his hard, muscular body. The thing about Nicky's cock is that it's so slightly curved to the left that it slides in and out, hitting the same spot perfectly each time. I shift my knees and start bouncing on top of him until my breasts are bouncing in his face. I tangle my hands in his hair, my lips inches from his, as his breathing picks up in heavy pants.

"Please, sir. Give it to me. I need it! Please," I whine, out of breath, as I hump him fast, my clit grazing his lower abs on every thrust.

"Hold still, pet. I want you to feel what you do to me," Nicky says with a hiss through his teeth, holding me tighter to his body until not even an inch separates us.

I shake, sweating, as I hold completely still and feel rope after thick rope of cum shots inside my pussy for a long while. I blink hard, feeling dizzy and giddy.

"I love you, Nicky. Your drive to succeed and protect those you love leaves me breathless. You inspire me to be better, to do better," I say in a husky voice, feeling emotions bubble up inside me. We've all been through so much.

"I love you too, Tillie. You're the type of woman I've always dreamed of having by my side." His eyes skim over my face before meeting my gaze with shiny eyes.

Dalton suddenly lifts my body off Nicky and into his arms while he reaches down to help his friend off the ground as we walk back over to where Cruz is hanging. Nicky doesn't say anything, just holding his hand out for the knife as he kneels down at Cruz's feet and takes his shoes off. Dom hands over the blade without complaint, looking grimly on as Nicky quickly cuts a thick line down Cruz's Achilles tendon. Cruz screams himself hoarse, his limbs jerking in pain as his blood flows out of each cut.

Dalton places a kiss on my shoulder, then sets me down in front of Cruz as he pushes me back on the ground until I'm on my hands and knees. I hear Dalton's pants unzip and feel the rough texture of his jeans against my sensitive skin. His big fingers drag through the cum mess around my pussy and thighs, collecting gushes of cum and circling it around my asshole until it's lubed up enough for him.

I take a deep inhale and don't breathe as I feel his fingers move away, and his cock takes place at my back entrance. I was looking down between my arms until Dalton's hand wrapped around my throat from behind and lifted my head up. My eyes connect with Cruz's cold, dead eyes. He can only feel anger, never love or sadness. I can see that now as he looks at me like he wants to murder me right now.

"Dalton?" I ask, not looking away as I address Dalton behind me as I spread my legs wider and arch my back.

"Yes, little bitch." I can hear the smile in his voice. He knows me so well and probably knows what I'm going to say.

"Daddy, please fuck my ass and make it hurt," I grunt out with a cry leaving my parted lips as Dalton shoves himself roughly past my burning ring of muscles and bottoms out inside of me.

He stays still for a second, letting me adjust until I give him a slight nod to move. He doesn't waste a second. His big, long cock slides out and dives right back in, just as hard. My knees scrape against the wood floor with each vicious thrust of Dalton's cock, making my body drag along the decking. His hips bounce off my ass as I move my hips, so I'm fucking him back. Tears leak down my face with each thrust of his body against mine. I know I will be sore later, but I wouldn't have it any other way. He grabs a handful of my ass cheeks and spreads them further apart to watch his cock disappear inside me. He groans loudly, the sound covering the noise of our skin slapping together, which grows louder and louder as he ruts into me like a wild animal.

I fucking love it. I crave the roughness. I need it or I just might die.

I honestly don't see Cruz in front of me anymore. He is a blur, and I couldn't care less that he's watching. I only care about Dalton's cock as it gives me a hard jerk in my ass, pulsing and expanding as he shoots his cum inside me with a roar.

"I love you, Dalton. I want to cuddle up with you and never leave. I know you'll always keep me warm inside and out," I gasp out, my arms shaking to hold me up as he slowly slides out of me with a deep breath.

"I love you too, Tillie. You couldn't get rid of me, even if you tried. You're stuck with me for life," Dalton grumbles huskily into my ear and pulls me to my feet, holding me to his side as he reaches for the waiting knife from Nicky's palm.

He doesn't even think about it, his expression giving nothing away as he jabs the blade down quickly and into Cruz's groin area. I've never heard a high-pitched scream like that before. His whole body shakes like he's seizing.

I stay still and remember this moment. I'm no longer afraid; my nightmare is coming to an end, and I can see a new beginning where I never have to run again.

Safe.

Loved.

It's like a switch flips in my head, a heavy burden lifted off my shoulder as I regard Cruz and step out of Dalton's embrace. I stand before him until he can only see me.

"I could never love you, Cruz. You are incapable of something that involves the heart. Love isn't just a feeling you think you have up here." I point to my head and then draw my fingers down to place them over my heart. "It's also right here. It's beating strong when you see that person smile for the first time. Their joy is your joy, happiness, sadness, anger... Everything you feel for them, they return the same feelings." I pause, swallowing the lump in my throat, and drag my hand further down until my fingertips graze my pussy.

I collect some of the cum there and draw my hand away to place it in front of his face, showing him the wetness and stickiness that's between my legs.

"I asked for this. I wanted it. I begged for them. That's consent and love. I could never give you that. I feel sorry for you. You'll never know what it feels like to love, and that's one thing that someone should experience at least once," I tell him, seeing he's holding onto every word I'm saying as his eyes go blank, no longer listening as he realizes I'm right.

"This is mercy from me. You deserve less, but I'm not you. Goodbye Cruz," I say, grabbing the knife Dalton hands me and placing it right over Cruz's heart, slowly putting pressure on the halt until the blade starts to sink into his flesh, pass tissue, veins, and finally into the beating muscle of his heart.

I don't look away. I watch the life bleed out of his eyes until he's gone for good. I step back, leaving the knife in his flesh where it belongs. No one says anything as Tey walks over to the control panel and messes with the switches until a grinding sound echoes into the night. I follow Cruz's body with my eyes as he moves over on the crane until his limp body is hovering over the deep, dark sea. I nod my head, knowing my men are watching my every move as they close in on me for support until I can only feel their warmth.

"Do it," I whisper and watch the crane release the hook. Cruz's body is suspended for a split second before he's dropped down into the ocean. I don't exhale until I hear the splash of his body hitting the water. Heavy sobs shake my chest as my eyes become blurry. I can't see who's touching me, but I know it's my guys offering their support and comfort.

It's finally over.

I can finally breathe for the first time in a long time.

"Can we go? I'm ready to go home," I say this into the night, huddling closer to my guys.

I want Tey's, Logan's, Dalton's, Nicky's, and Dom's arms wrapped around me in our bed. I want to lay around in bed with them because nothing calls us away, and I want to just sleep for a long time—dreamless sleep.

Finally. It's over.

Rig

I stare at the TV hanging on the wall in the corner, the news station about to start its live coverage of tonight's six o'clock news. I reach for the remote attached to my bedside and mute the TV just before I weakly sink into the hospital bed while closing my eyes. It's been a blur ever since last night.

I take that back; it's been a blur for a few years. Ever since that little fucking shit, Cruz, has drugged me and left me at a psychiatric hospital. Some days, I'm not sure if what I'm seeing in front of me is real or not. I am still drugged up and stuck in a wheelchair in front of my patient bedroom with only a view of the forest, or did Cruz really pull me out? Did he take me away from the horrible place he threw me in, or did he stop those god-awful drugs only to torture me once I was lucid with the knowledge my daughter was raped by the club? I used to call those men my brothers, and they did the most horrendous thing a father never wants to hear about his own kid. My memory is foggy most days. At times, I thought I was hallucinating Cruz coming for a visit and telling stories about my Tillie. It felt like an endless nightmare that just kept coming back to haunt me.

Since the moment I was weaned off the pharmaceutical drugs, the side effects haven't been pleasant, but it's the least I deserve. I've failed my Tillie as a father, the one person who was supposed to protect her. I wake up with a fever most days, shivering but running hot. My skin feels extra sensitive, and the hospital bedsheets feel itchy. The full-body jerks out of nowhere will probably never go away; the muscle spasms wake me up in the middle of the night, though sometimes that's a good thing. I shut my eyes and only see her sweet, sixteen-year-old face—so innocent to the world around her.

God. I've failed so much. I should have gotten her out sooner.

I inhale a shaky breath, licking my dry lips, and open my eyes to reach weakly for my water on the bedside table. My hand pauses midair as my gaze locks on the brown eyes staring at me from the open doorway. I feel like my heart is going to pound out of my chest. The wires hooked up to the hospital machines tell their own story of what I'm feeling as the heart monitor starts to go crazy.

"Rig," she whispers, her bottom lip trembling as she slowly steps into the room warily but freezes when she sees me trying to sit up in my bed but keep failing.

I'm weak, only skin and bones from years of starving and living off drugs. I fall back on the hospital bed with a shaky exhale and a small coughing fit. She stares at me like a deer in headlights, hardly blinking as she stands halfway in the door and one foot out. My eyes fill with tears as I raise one arm hesitantly, not knowing if she will want to be hugged by me after I've abandoned her.

"Dad," she chokes out with a sob leaving her lips and quickly crosses the room, which feels like miles away, until my Tillie is in my arms, finally.

"I'm sorry, Til. So sorry." I feel my throat close as tears fill my eyes. My little girl is hugging me back as if she'll never let go.

She climbs onto the bed and curls up to my side, squeezing me so tight as if afraid to let go. I return the feeling. I'm so scared this is a dream, and I'm going to wake up with my arms empty and Tillie far, far away.

"No. I knew you didn't just leave me. I knew it," she sobs into my chest, her shoulders shaking as I hold her with my head resting on top of hers while tears trail down my cheeks.

"I'll never leave you again, pumpkin," I rasp out and just hold my daughter as she cries years of pain.

We don't say anything for a while; just absorbing this is real. I can hear nurses and the machines of other patients out in the hall, and I can hear the sound of my Tillie's wrecking sobs dying down after a while. I can only blink slowly at the TV, not really seeing the news, but my attention is pulled away from a male throat clearing from the doorway. Tillie sniffles and leans up to sit up on the edge of the bed but refuses to let go of my hand.

"Hey. I have coffee," a man says, holding up crappy hospital coffee, and steps inside as Tillie smiles at him and holds out her hand.

I watch him warily, squeezing Tillie's hand as he reaches my bedside, and it clicks why he looks so familiar as his light brown eyes connect with mine. He was there last night, even though it's all fuzzy around the edges for me, but I remember his fear for my daughter as he lost his shit and threw a chair out a window.

Logan. That's his name.

"Dad." Tillie looks at me, watching me watch her boyfriend with narrowed eyes. It's something I can't help.

My daughter has been hurt too much in life in such a

short time. I'm about to open my mouth to tell him to give us a few minutes of privacy so I can ask her if she's safe, but that one word stops me.

Dad.

My heart rate picks up as my eyes burn. I refuse to cry in front of this punk boyfriend of hers, but damn if hearing that come out of her mouth doesn't cause me to melt in warmth. I've always wanted her to call me dad, to know that my blood runs through hers, but fear held me back for a long time. The unknown of what Payne would do if he found out scared me more than anything. Where would we go? Would she want to leave? I had those questions and held off until I felt it was the right time, but I was too late.

"Rig. Dad." Tillie scoots closer, setting her coffee on my bedside table, and grabs my hands in both of hers. "I want you to know I don't blame you for anything. I knew you wouldn't leave me behind. For a while, I thought you were dead. I want you to know that I'm happy to call you Dad. It's all I've ever wanted."

"Fuck, Til," I rasp out and cover her hands with mine with a squeeze. "I wish I could have gotten you out sooner. I thought I had time; I should have run away with you, kid, and never looked back, just like your mother did." I shake my head in regret and side-eye her boyfriend as he remains quiet but watches everything like a hawk.

"I know. I wouldn't have gone, I don't think. I thought the club would always be my home. I thought they were family, so I would have fought with you to stay. I know this. I can't turn back time, but I don't think I would if I could. I'm meant to be here." My strong daughter says with a hand squeeze before she releases me and gestures with a smile to Logan.

"I know who he is. The man who likes throwing chairs

out of windows and losing his damn mind over my daughter," I rasp out, reaching shakily for my water again, and take a sip as I watch Logan shuffle on his feet and place his hands in his pants pockets in a nervous habit. "Thank you."

He freezes, not expecting that, but narrows his gaze with suspicion until he sees how sincere I am. He nods and rocks on his heels before turning his attention to the TV.

A silent man with haunted eyes has seen shit in life; I recognize that look. I don't care what he's done in life. So long as he treats my daughter right, then I don't care about anything else. The same goes for the rest of her men; I won't ask just yet. I don't think I'm ready for that answer. Maybe after all the side effects of drugs leave my body, I can gain some of my strength back so I can kick some ass if need be.

"Can you turn up the volume?" Logan asks, pointing at the TV with scrunched brows as he reads the headlines.

I grab the remote and unmute the TV as Tillie turns on the edge of the bed to see the TV as well.

"This is five o'clock news. Reporter Elle Jones here, covering tonight's devastating yet heroic story of our city's beloved Captain Russo. I think it's going to go down in history that Franco Russo was a hero to this city. He helped uncover a drug bust, the biggest we have ever seen in Los Angeles, but unfortunately, it led to his death. Captain Russo was shot by Jin Hino, none other than the supplier of cocaine and heroin. This has been an investigation for years, and it has finally come to an end. Luckily, Jin Hino has passed away, was shot on the scene in a shootout, and ended up being the biggest drug lord in our city. Today, we will honor Captain Russo for saving our city. His funeral will be held this Friday at Welderington Cemetery," Elle Jones drones on and on about Franco Russo's great accomplishment, but I'm hardly paying attention as Tillie and Logan make eye contact with some emotion I can't place.

He looks sad but relieved, I think.

Logan clears his throat and glances away before turning his gaze back to me with a determined glint.

"Sir. If you are looking for a place to stay—I mean, if you would want to stay—" Logan rubs the back of his neck, his cheeks turning red as he struggles for words, and he looks at Tillie, who is trying really hard not to smile.

"Well, spit it out. How are you supposed to date my daughter if you can't even ask me to stay with you guys?" I grunt out, crossing my arms over my chest and raising an eyebrow in challenge, which only has his eyes hardening into a glare.

"I insist you stay with us. There is plenty of room at Dom's home. We won't take no for an answer, but we can't make you stay if you don't want to. The offer stands." Logan shrugs and tries to look like he doesn't care one way or another, but he keeps looking at my daughter, searching for approval from her.

That's the look of a man in love.

"I think I'll take you up on that. I want to be near my daughter. We have a lot to catch up on." I smile at Tillie as she shakes her head with a chuckle but blinks rapidly to hold back tears.

Like I said before, she's so fucking strong. That's my girl.

"I'd love that, Dad," she says, wiping at a tear, and smiles happily up at Logan.

"Me too, but I do have a question," I say slowly, pretending to be confused as I furrow my brows together.

"What is it?" she replies, her smile dropping slightly in worry.

"Who's Dom?" I hold back a chuckle as her eyes widen,

and a blush stains her cheeks as she looks everywhere but at me.

I don't need to worry about her anymore, I think. She looks like she's in good hands, and that is enough for me to see her happy. I'll take my time getting to know the woman before me. I'm just getting to know my daughter.

We'll need to have that talk about our pasts one day, all the pain and happiness that came along the way to here and now.

One step at a time.

It's all I have now... time.

I can't wait to learn who my daughter is.

My daughter.

EPILOGUE

Tillie

ou know, it's not like the movies at all.

I don't have a sudden urge to run through a field of wildflowers and act like it's my first time seeing the sun as I reach my hands to the sky.

I'm not going to scream at the top of my lungs that I'm free if I were on the back of Dalton's bike as the wind makes a tangled mess of my hair.

I wanted freedom from my old life, which seemed impossible to escape.

Doris once told me I'd soar one day, blinding everyone as they saw me fly into the sunshine.

I held those words to heart, thinking that's all I needed to do.

Run.

I kept running until my feet lifted off the ground as I chased freedom.

But the reality is that my feet are firmly planted, and I don't plan on going anywhere.

I think this is what happiness feels like. Content.

Being loved and cared for.

"What are you thinking about so hard over here, baby

girl?" Logan asks in the shell of my ear as he sneaks up behind me.

"If it's possible to feel like my heart will burst full of love, but if it's okay to feel sad," I reply truthfully, leaning my back against his front for a second.

"Everyone feels sad, Tillie. No one walks around happily all the time. It's okay to not smile all the time. We all have our days," he says, his voice deep and serious as he presses a kiss on my shoulder blade and strides away to give me time to think.

I've been processing. Still am.

Since leaving my past behind and looking forward, it's been... difficult to come to terms with the fact that I no longer have to look over my shoulders anymore.

Three days ago, I locked myself up in our room, staring at the ceiling and wondering, What now?

The guys checked on me but gave me space. Maybe they could see the confused, lost look on my face. Or the need to have a minute to myself. Either way, I love them even more for giving me time to deal. I finally decided that enough is enough, and it's time to start living how I want to live. The past won't hold me in its tight grasp anymore. I choose what I want without worrying about that little scared girl in the corner of my mind making an appearance. I let myself go.

I told the old me that it's okay now.

We can move on.

With that peaceful feeling of letting it all lay down to rest, I can finally breathe without my breath catching in the back of my throat.

I get out of bed.

I shower and put my clothes on.

I walk slowly into the living room and out the back door

onto the white-sand beaches without feeling like the whole weight of the world was on my shoulders.

It's how I found myself, with my head tilted back and smiling as the sun warmed my skin. I slowly open my eyes to take in the scene before me.

Nicola and Evan are lounging under enormous umbrellas as they lay on their sides to stare into each other's eyes. They both look so happy and in love. They deserve to be two young people in love, free to love who they want without fear. I shake my head as they start making out and gaze around until I see Nicky further down the beach under another huge umbrella, but his facial expression has me smiling.

He's staring at his sister with a disgusted, curled lip. He looks a little green, but I can see how his eyes soften as his sister giggles. He can pretend all he wants, but I think he likes Evan, too. He's good for Nicola.

Two shouts and splashes pull my gaze away to see Dalton charging after Tey, who is giggling like a manic schoolgirl, as he runs into the ocean with a drenched Dalton stomping after him in the sand. I hope Tey never changes— that he keeps pulling pranks and just being his cute, psycho self. I love that Dalton looks like this total badass biker but is a big softy inside. It's like having my own giant personal teddy bear. I bite my lip to hold in my giggles as Dalton literally picks up Tey over his head and throws him into the ocean, landing with a big splash.

I turn my head and look over my shoulder as I hear Dom and Logan arguing as they walk down the steps over to us. They might never admit it, but they've become really close over the last six months, bonding over pain and what-ifs. They really are more alike than they think. Both are so strong, stubborn, and protective to the point of driving me crazy sometimes, but I wouldn't have it any other way. They might be besties at this point, and I wonder who will admit it first.

A throat clearing has me peering to the left and down as my dad stares at me with a pointed look. I'm caught and busted again for staring a little too long at my men, but I won't deny it. I just shrug with a smile and continue to check out my guys. Rig just rolls his eyes with a grunt as usual and stretches out in his beach recliner, returning to his reading with a small smile. It's good to see him happy and relaxed. He hasn't once brought up Diana, and neither have I. She's disappeared, and I hope she stays that way. I won't have her coming into my life and turning her nose up at me. Or hurting Rig, he has a good heart and forgives easily; he only wants the best for those around him.

God. This must be heaven.

I sat in the pain, stuck for a long time, and felt torment down to the very depths of my soul.

Maybe... just maybe, this is my soul healing, or at least the depraved parts mending back together until I'm just pieces held together by a thin thread.

I'll fall again, but this time, I have psycho boyfriends to pick me up when I can't get up myself.

This is me.

Tillie.

Five dangerous men captured my heart and didn't let go.

And the ending I used to wish for... well, it's taken a turn to a bright, bloody, and a little crazy future.

I can't wait to see what my beginning has in store for me.

The End

ACKNOWLEDGMENTS

I can't believe it. Three years with these characters living rent-free in my head and their story is finally finished. I hope my dear readers are happy with this ending and don't cry too much. I was balling my eyes out even during the sex scenes. It's been an emotional ride, but I'm so glad I pushed that publish button with book one... I almost didn't.

Thank you! Thank you so much for sticking with me and loving these punks just as much as I do. I couldn't have done this without you guys!

I want to give a huge shout-out to my Alpha and Beta team for helping. Your advice and comments kept me going. I appreciate you guys so much! Claire and Brittany, thank you for coming in hot and hyping me up to finish this book. Sam and Mandy, I've made you two my ride-or-die bitches so get used to it. You can't leave me.

Freaking Penn Cassidy for being my hype girl and letting me rant my frustrations at these characters sometimes being buttheads, I love ya, girl. Thank you for being an amazing friend.

Last, to my supportive husband who listened to my random ramblings at one o'clock in the morning and nodded like you understood what I was talking about even though you were confused as hell. I love you for being here for me and making me chase my dreams.

STALKING LINKS FOR MADELINE FAY

http://www.madelinefayauthor.com

ABOUT MADELINE FAY

Madeline lives in rural Michigan in a castle with all her fur babies and her lovely husband. She loves to read, you'll find her in her tower with her kindle and drinking boba tea or coffee.

She has a few addictions, chocolate is her weakness and fanfiction Dramione.

She likes to pretend she's a main character in a Korean drama and listens to K-pop as she dances around the house.

Her brain never stops creating conversations with WIP characters... you should see her Google Drive. It's ridiculous how many tabs are opened for new stories to write.

She's a zombie half the time during the day until the coffee kicks in but at night she watches over her city in the shadows and calls herself Batman.

Not really but she keeps hoping it might come true one day.

She's in her bat cave writing and plotting mad, evil genius stories while sipping some wine.